GENITAL GRINDER

RYAN HARDING

deadite
press

DEADITE PRESS
205 NE BRYANT
PORTLAND, OR 97211
www.DEADITEPRESS.com

AN ERASERHEAD PRESS COMPANY
www.ERASERHEADPRESS.com

ISBN: 1-62105-022-X

Printed in the USA.

ACKNOWLEDGEMENTS

Thank you to all who wanted this collection, in particular Jeff Burk of Deadite and Brian Keene for putting him in contact with me. And to Edward Lee for the killer foreword and just for being a cool guy to me over the years, in addition to consistently raising the disgust quotient of his fiction. The morbid among us find this a true inspiration.

A very special thank you to Bob Strauss, Bill Hughes, and Darrin McDonel (and his dad) for playing archaeologist for me and excavating stories and fragments lost to me for years.

My gratitude to my past editors and publishers – Matt Schwartz (Horrornet), Dave Barnett (Necro Publications), Kelly Laymon and Jeremy Lassen (Freak Press), Eddie McMullen, Jr./Feo Amante, Bill Hughes again (Dread: Tales of the Uncanny and Grotesque), Sandra Fritz (Altered Perceptions) and Mikhail and The Meat Socket.

To my collaborators over the years – Brent Zirnheld, James Futch, James Newman, Geoff Cooper (duuuuuuuude) and the other co-contributors to Darker Dawning 1 and 2: Regina Mitchell, BK, Mike Oliveri, Mikey Huyck, John Urbancik, and the inimitable GAK.

The YKOF partners in chyme of today and yore.

And to Harry Bennett, Suzzan Blac (for the sickening art), Mike Bracken, Bill Connolly, Simon Clark, Jay Clarke/ Michael Slade, Laura Elvin, Jamey Fiala, Brad Hodson (quim!), Jack Ketchum, Ann Laymon, R. Murphy, John Pelan and Will Rahmer.

In memory of J.G. Ballard, Richard Laymon, and Rex Miller.

CONTENTS

ENJOY THE GANG RAPE
BY EDWARD LEE

Quite a number of years ago—at least 15, but my aging gray matter can't be sure—I was contacted by a fan named Ryan Harding. I've always tried to respond to all fan contacts (every now and then, however, you get an obvious clunker, like the ex-con who wrote to tell me The Bighead's most violent scenes provided him with superb masturbation fodder; or the woman who wanted to know if I'd like to see pictures of her cutting herself—these, yes, are such clunkers. It is advisable for an author *never* to reply to these red flags) and I was impressed as well as flattered by Mr. Harding's generous words regarding my work; additionally, he bestowed such words in a manner and air which disclosed a formidable command of the language and a most arresting and cogent creative bent. Moreover, Mr. Harding was a positive acquaintance of several friends of mine; hence, it seemed unlikely that he might be hiding "clunkerdom" beneath a clever camouflage and would later stalk me or, say, start murdering people in ways which duplicated the superfluity of murders in my books. So I chose to pursue correspondence with this young, intelligent, and spirited Mr. Harding. He had aspirations of becoming a writer himself, and flattered me further via the declaration that I was an influence of some significance to him. Then, one day, he asked me if I'd care to read some of his song lyrics—he was into Metal as was I, so I said "sure." The prospect seemed enticing: I was very curious what this bright, new-generation

7

individual might demonstrate in the way of creative verse; indeed, it struck me as an attractive occasion to observe the tenor of such an enthusiast's muse, and, doubly, I wondered just what might be the *products* of that muse?

Well. Here is an inventory of those products. Psychosis. Misogyny. Misanthropy. Nihilism. Sadism. Necrophily. Erotopathy. Profanation. Alienation. Blasphemy. And every manner of irreverence, aberrant impulse, and outright *satanism* conceivable and inconceivable.

I've long since lost these lyrics (or perhaps I deleted them for fear that their negativity might plunge me into a abysm of clinical depression!), but I recall—and suspect I always will—the final line: "We fucked her good, my knife and I."

Wow, I thought, *this guy's really fucked up in the head,* and then I felt suddenly leery when I appended my conjecture, *Wow, this guy's even more fucked up in the head than ME.*

Gore-house smut, enmity personified, and scatology in grand style proved the common denominators hovering amid Harding's aesthetic elan, and certainly we've seen a *whole lot* of such stuff infiltrating the sub-genre known (among other appellations) as Extreme Horror. Ninety percent of the work is probably worthy of the critical lambasting it receives. Grossness for the sake of grossness. Amateur scribes merely heaping revolting images and disorganized, just-popped-into-my-head scenes of unlikely violence upon the page without any regard to integration, character, story-line. "The bitch screamed as the maggot-ridden zombie rammed its rotten cock into her gaping, reeking pussy and came spurts of pus!" That kind of shit, and personally I'm sick to death of it, as have many readers been for a long time. One time I recall a critic referring to "Extreme Horror" as something akin to a little boys' circle-jerk club wherein the purpose of each participant is to try to gross the next guy out. I actually quite agree with that (though accurately or inaccurately I *disagree* that I am a member of that self-same club!) because it appears that what Extreme Horror at large lacks most of all is a discipline of craft. It's just gross-out sex and gross-out violence that the misguided author thinks will gross the reader out. But it *doesn't* gross the reader out. It *bores* the reader. To tears. And it not only sullies the popular impression of the genre as a whole, but makes the more serious authors out there look just as inept, just as juvenile, and just as I-don't-give-a-shit.

Which brings us back to Monsieur Harding.

He's not part of the "club," folks. He gives a shit-and-a-half about not only the speculative and/or societal points of extreme fiction but also the very *craft* of it. Over time I read much of Harding's works-in-progress, mostly stories but also some novel partials, and in them not only did I find those previously stated thematic denominators (gore-house smut, enmity personified, and scatology in grand style) but also a nearly "Strunk-and-White" obsession with prose-mechanics, stylistic feature-through-discipline, charactorial integration, and plot dynamics. It quickly occurred to me that Ryan Harding had (and, furthermore, *has*) the tenacity, know-how, and wherewithal to become a very potent practitioner in the field of Extreme Horror. Here's a writer who regards the venue as something rife with value, relevance, and, indeed, meaning. It's a gore-house world, folks. Just read the paper. This globe is aswarm with enmity personified. (Did you see Daniel Pearl's beheading?) Scatology in grand style is as real as the mouse button which clicks interested pervertos and other reprobate scum to websites offering bestiality, sex with the severely handicapped, vid-clips of crack-addicted women eating feces ice-cream cones or consuming fish bowls of semen, spit-fights, nose-blow bukkake, animal torture, galleries of deformed children, vomit-swap buffets, etc., *ad infinitum.*

Ah! The real world!

It's that same world, too, that Harding's fiction seeks to delineate in a manner unique unto itself. Some of the stories in this book make notorious writers like, say, Peter Sotos and celebrated madmen as, say, Jeffery Dahmer look like "the veriest tyros," (to steal a cool simile from Lovecraft). There are times as well when they make, say, Edward Lee, look like, say, a baby in a high chair and making ga-ga noises.

Likewise, some of the imagery herein is more disturbing, despair-summoning, and stomach-upheaving than any I've read anywhere.

Allow me to make an abstraction—granted, a goofy one probably—or perhaps a "figurative representation" is a better way to put it. As a reader of Harding's work, I'd like you to imagine that your psyche is a vagina.

That's right. A vagina.

What Harding's work provides for you is a raucous, down and dirty, butt-stinky gang-bang with a multitude of demented and very horny participants. You are humped and humped and humped by Harding's fiction; you are prodded, poked, skewered, and penetrated time and time again; you are stuffed like a turkey, pounded like sod, and plungered like a gas station toilet. (Man, oh, man! You sure got more than you bargained for in *this* gang-bang, huh? Ho!) Your suitors, I'll add, don't like you at all; in fact, they *hate* you, they hate you for no reason at all. They don't give two diddlies about you, nor two shits. You're not a person, you're not an individual consciousness. What you are to *this* miscreant crew is nothing more than a hot hole for their penises to have a party in. And there are many such penises, and some come back for a double-dip. Ah, but it's not *typical* sperm that you're being filled like a cannoli with. See, each ejaculation comes possessed of an exclusive constituent, and those constituents are as follows:

Psychosis. Misogyny. Misanthropy. Nihilism. Sadism. Necrophily. Erotopathy. Profanation. Alienation. Blasphemy. And every manner of irreverence, aberrant impulse, and outright *satanism* conceivable and inconceivable.

Yes.

Now the gang-bang is over. Your suitors are gone, leaving you sore, stupefied, and full of evil sperm. When you get home, you douche at once, intent to flush it all out, but the more you douche, the more you seem to push all that devilish slop *deeper*. Will you ever get it all out? But at least the nightmare is over, right?

Wrong. Five weeks later you find out you're pregnant.

That's what Harding's work will do to you. It will turn you into a *tramp*. It will transfigure you into an *object* for *use*—a *receptacle* for all the animus, loathe, and maleficence the human mind has generated, a *drain-can* for the filth of all the abominations of the earth, and then? It will *knock you up*.

These are my introspective impressions of Harding's fiction. He means business. He's not simply trying to gross us out—he's trying to make us *see*. (And I suppose any of us who happen to see *ourselves* . . . well, then, such persons are in a heap of trouble!)

So enjoy the tour, friends. Enjoy the gang-bang. You may need psych drugs afterwards, you may need an air-sick bag and a steam shower, but I feel confident that you will be provocatively moved by this book.

Edward Lee
August 9, 2011

DAMAGED GOODS

"I'm telling you," Greg said to Von, "it's Sarah Pensie."

Von shook his head, not believing it for a second. Sarah Pensie—who graduated two years ahead of Von and three years before Greg dropped out— had moved to Hollywood to become a star and wound up discovering her true calling in life: the go-to girl for "butt stuff" in the adult film industry, known as "Lolita Ream." It was rumored that she did specialty porn in addition to the mainstream stuff Von had actually seen, and supposedly her biggest underground hit was called *Anal Halfpipe*, wherein she gave a burly truck-driver an enema. The ejected suds were then used to wash out her slut-filthy mouth.

Therefore, it was rather unlikely that the corpse prone on tarp in Von's basement—an eleven hour drive from the P.O. box for her fan club—was Sarah Pensie. They hadn't stripped her just yet, probably because they couldn't believe she was there (whoever *she* was).

It had been an otherwise routine night for them. They'd spent the usual ninety minutes rooting through the dumpster outside the gynecological clinic searching for discarded latex gloves and sanitary napkins. Homeward bound and playing a game of their own creation—"I Wonder Whose Cooze?"— they'd found the woman splattered on Sherman Avenue (and a few pieces here and there on Bowling Boulevard).

A hit-and-run, probably. Figuring that police probably hadn't been notified yet, Von and Greg quickly loaded her

13

up into the truck-bed and peeled out for home. They now examined her on blue canvas under the fluorescent lights of Von's basement.

Her left eyeball dangled precariously on a cheekbone peeking through her skin, a stringy optic nerve straining to hold on. Her nose hooked unnaturally to the right, which made Von think she could advertise for that breakfast cereal with the dumbass bird—*Toucan Sam,* he remembered—if the dried cluster of blood and snot was wiped away. The right eye was completely gone, probably still on Bowling Boulevard. A few brain fragments dangled from the socket. Her limbs were contorted in a fashion more suitable for broken toothpicks than arms or legs. Her white novelty shirt reading BUILT TO LAST was all but obscured by smears of blood, and the story with her jeans wasn't all that different. She'd either vomited just before or right at the moment of impact, undigested debris and bile testifying to a Mexican dinner. She probably should have been slamming a Slim-Fast shake, because the bitch was well on her the way to maximum density. They had broken a mean sweat lugging her to the truck bed on Sherman, so Von sure hoped she thought about the plight of her pallbearers when she made out her will.

Von now let himself dare to believe this was all for real. He couldn't begin to fathom what altruistic gesture he might have made for the universe to reward him with a gift like this—free *puss,* for the love of God, left out for any takers like a suave leather couch at curbside trash pick up . . . a suave leather couch you could *cornhole*—but he'd gladly accept it with his warmest regards. Short of Ed McMahon dropping by to hand him a check for a million bucks, he realized this might be the luckiest day of his life. Fixing on the ruined body, he savored the moment a few beats longer, even while melancholy at the possibility that after tonight *nothing* may ever compare to this. It even seemed almost *wrong* on some strange metaphysical level to get down to the business of actually *defiling* her, but he recognized this for the craziness it was. He wasn't delusional . . . this dead woman was getting shot full of his ball sauce, thank you very much.

They stripped her down. Their hands were soon sticky not only from the blood but from pushing in a few lengths of small intestine and miscellaneous vital organs spilling through a tear in her belly like detritus through a burst trash bag. Von was more than happy to let Greg single-handedly remove her underwear. About every excretion and fluid possible had turned her panties into multiple Rorschach tests. He winced a little when Greg held them up, the perineal area carrying some added weight. What Von didn't know was that Greg hadn't lost his janitorial job at Bartok General Hospital due to downsizing, like he'd said. No, security had filmed him creeping into the coma ward and consuming whatever he found in colostomy bags. Lightning struck twice soon after, Greg once more "downsized" for lapping up reproductive fluid from the rubber sheets of mental patients. If Von had seen *Busted on the Job 7* and *8* on Fox, he would have known the sickening truth.

Von's eyes jumped a little. "Whoa . . . Houston, we have a problem."

"What's wrong?"

"Take a look."

Greg set the underwear down for future inspection and indulgence beside her purse (Liz Claiborne, as were the high heels twenty yards further down Sherman) and turned. It didn't take him long to see what had spooked Von. Genital warts stared back at him, an algae of shame which had burst open in a few places due to one or another of the night's mishaps. If for some reason he hadn't seen them, his nose would have notified him quickly enough. The reek of the mucus-like fluid raped his olfactory senses right up the ass.

"Damn, Von . . . that's almost enough to make a man reconsider."

"You speak the gospel, Greg; it really is *almost* enough. But given we're a couple of resourceful bad-asses, help me flip over Orca here and we'll try plan B."

Plan B wasn't much better. Von felt like pointing out

the obvious, so he said, "She's got a bunch of black beetles crawling out of her asshole."

"You see!" Greg shouted. "I *told* you it was Sarah Pensie!"

Von decided he didn't want to know exactly why this observation legitimized Greg's theory, and didn't ask. He grabbed a can of Raid off a nearby workbench and sprayed about half of it into the infested orifice. Insecticide and vaginal befoulment battled for olfactory prevalence in the confines of the basement.

This couldn't be very sanitary, but you only live once.

Von didn't want to look a gift horse in the mouth, and he was still ever most thankful for this apparently sexually adventurous bounty bestowed upon them, but this particular gem had admittedly lost a little luster beneath the jeweler's magnifying glass. He decided he could afford to savor a bit longer, maybe give his senses a bit longer to acclimate to the godforsaken reek.

Von clapped Greg on the shoulder. "Suit up and go to war, soldier."

Greg gave him a thumb-up, obviously trying not to breathe in. "Lock and load."

He started unbuckling his pants. Von didn't necessarily want to be around to witness what was going to happen, but he didn't trust her alone with Greg.

He was going to at least busy himself with other pursuits when something caught his eye: Greg's asshole looked incredibly chafed and swollen. Von tried not to let his gaze linger, but the image haunted. It solved many a mystery— why Greg had been squirming in his seat all night and the probable truth behind why he'd curiously asked to borrow Von's toilet brush a couple days ago.

I keep pretty sick company, Von thought, opening the woman's purse. *Look at him.* Sodomizing himself with household utensils was just the tip of the iceberg. The crazy bastard wasn't even wearing a condom.

Von opened her wallet, trying to ignore the grunts and Greg's awkward breathing, apparently searching for the air of least resistance. Triumph soared in Von's breast. "Hey, Greg, I told you it wasn't Sarah Pensie! It's just some whore named Claire Perkins."

Greg finished his tenure in Claire's ass, then pulled out so quickly that he lost equilibrium and slid backwards on the floor. "Claire Perkins!" he yelled. "Man, it's a good thing I chose the backdoor—this bitch is my cousin! I wouldn't have felt right about sticking her box."

Von snorted. "*Well*. Let a real man show you what it's all about. Help me get her face-up again."

They rolled her again. Von took a grease rag off a work bench and tried to clear the runway. Her chancres gave way and burst beneath the cloth, soaking through to his fingers. It felt like popping the bubblewrap cushioning a package. A mantra ran through his mind each time another sore exploded: "*It's okay, I have a condom . . . It's okay, I have a condom . . . It's okay, I have a condom ...*"

The prize he uncovered admittedly wasn't worth the effort. He'd seen raw hamburger at McDonald's more fetching than this. Beggars can't be choosers, he thought. He slipped on the condom and eased into her—*carefully* putting his weight down, lest he incite more chancres to revolt. It occurred to him that wading into a kiddie pool full of cottage cheese wouldn't be very different from this.

No, damn it, NO!

It was too much, as he feared it would be. He flashed on a hundred grotesque images to try to hold off the combustion, but they only seemed to rally the dam-bursting sensation in his scrotum. His condom was instantly filled to the brim.

Von took a razor and carved out Claire's asshole five minutes later, amidst many wet sounds like a kid goose-stepping on slushy snow. With a little effort he slid the excised anus around his member. "You weren't kidding, Greg," he proclaimed. "Fits like a glove!"

It cheered him up instantly. Now it was just a matter of waiting to get hard again.

"I'm gonna fix me a sandwich," he said. "You want one?"

"Is a pig's ass pork?" Greg replied.

17

"Be right back." Von scaled the basement steps, growing accustomed to the feel of Claire's ass bound around him. He extracted some sandwich meat from the fridge with the appropriate condiments, as well as some French bread. Halfway through completing his task, he figured he should wash his hands.

As he dried them off, a siren went off in his head—he'd left Greg alone with the body. He crept down the stairs far enough to where he could get a quick look-see at how Greg had chosen to occupy himself. Von silently cursed his carelessness as he watched.

Greg had further slit open Claire's belly with a box cutter and yanked out her bladder. He now held it over his head as he ran it through with the knife, each gouge showering him with another yellow stream in a postmortem golden shower.

Von steamed. Bad enough the son of a bitch had crammed that toilet brush up his ass God knew how many times—no, he'd had to damage that most blessed of gifts, something that would *never* simply fall into Von's lap again as long as he lived. He could practically feel part of his soul die forever in that moment. If the universe had been sizing them up to make this whole ultra convenient hit-and-run recovery thing a regular gig, Greg had singlehandedly proven them both unworthy forever. You make the most of damaged goods; you don't corrupt them.

Von went back to the kitchen and undid his jeans. He opened Greg's sandwich and slid his meat between the bread and fixings. He was uncircumcised, and an appreciable amount of pud butter was still congealing in his foreskin. Von solved the problem by wiping it clean on the bread, then patted it shut.

Greg tried to act like nothing had happened while Von was away, the bladder held behind his back as if his mysterious outbreak of liquid jaundice wasn't a pulsing neon sign. Von passed him the sandwich, thinking, *Can't have a submarine without semen now, can we?* That a bodily excretion inside of an edible Trojan horse might be like water off a duck's back to his friend—the guy who had just moments ago cornholed his dead cousin and slashed open her bladder like it would yield scented bath oils—never occurred to him.

He heard a sound like a washcloth being dropped in the bathtub. It was Claire's bladder hitting the back wall as Greg tried to ditch the evidence. A bovine look of innocence plastered on his face, Greg took a heroic bite out of his contaminated sandwich, sinewy strands of meat pulling taut and snapping as he tore away, a token *Mmmmmmmm!* as his compliment to the chef. If Von hadn't been looking for the wince of disgust on his pal's face, he might have missed it. Greg never missed a beat, nodding as he chewed, eyes slightly watery.

This, along with another joy-buzz, restored Von's good mood.

He was hard again.

SHARING NEEDLES

JOURNAL ENTRY, JANUARY 21

Where does something like this begin? You wake up every day and ask yourself how it became what it is and you always come back to fantasy. This kind of fantasizing, though . . . it doesn't suddenly happen. It isn't like those dreams in the womb, images from a life you haven't even begun. Or at least it doesn't seem that way.

So you ask yourself—why the fantasies?

You immediately think of the magazines. They were in a box in the attic, guarded by the torso of a mannequin. The attic light bulb burned out sometime after Christmas and had not been replaced by summer. You were bored enough to look around anyway. No school and all your friends were on vacation, so you got adventurous. It was early afternoon and the sun was as bright as a camera flash through the only window.

It indicated the box.

That's what you thought years later. You were meant to find the box and the heavens conspired to make sure you did. You opened it and then sat down in the surrounding pool of light, as though the pull of gravity was greatly concentrated in that one special area.

Ironically a good deal of the magazines you found were issues of Life, *although many of the images on the cover were devoted to the antithesis of its namesake.*

Death triumphant.

20

Death, the king.

The War to End All Wars.

You didn't really care about this, though. School was in a few weeks, you'd hear plenty of it then. The other magazines you found, though . . . you weren't going to hear Ms. Garza talk about them in a classroom. Not ever.

Time had not been especially kind to them. The pages were yellowed and slight water damage left waves on some of the covers. They looked like comic books at first, which might have been interesting anyway, but then you saw they were something else. They bore the title SHOCKING DETECTIVE. *The covers were illustrated, united by a theme similar to the* Life *coverage of the War to End All Wars.*

The theme was women.

Women in various stages of undress.

Women in peril.

They all looked like Hollywood starlets who lived in the same apartment building. They could have been sisters, these redheads, brunettes, and blondes. They were all beautiful, they were all voluptuous, they were all terrified— their mouths set in a silent scream that seemed to resound far beyond the barriers of the page.

They all had male visitors.

Men with masks and black gloves.

Men with knives.

You were initially disappointed when you opened these issues of Shocking Crimes *and discovered they weren't illustrated after all; only the covers were artistically rendered. You were still interested enough to read them, though, even if there was going to be plenty of* that *in school, too.*

Who could have resisted the allure of the articles, though? Such titles! "Madman Mutilated the Missouri Mother!" "Sadist Slaughtered Six Southern Belles!" "Fiend Filleted Aunt Frieda!"

The promise didn't stop there. Even a cursory glance of the articles revealed several highlighted captions throughout which presented the horror in bigger letters and bolder print. For instance:

"Her husband of fifteen years couldn't even recognize her. Several blows to her face and an aborted attempt to burn her remains resulted in damage too extensive for identification. 'You'd never believe that twisted mass of burnt decay was ever a human being,' said coroner Brad Zeller."

But not to be outdone by:

"The murder weapon was obviously an axe. There were deep grooves consistent with overhead swings of said instrument in sixteen wounds on her body. There were also footprint indentations on her rib cage, as though the killer stood on her to help him withdraw the axe so that he could swing it again . . . and again . . . and again."

They were always crimes of passion, if not necessarily in the traditional sense. This wasn't about retribution because of a cheating wife. This was something deeper. You understood that then, even if you could never have verbalized it. This was about a sacred drama, scenes from a ritual unfolding in unremarkable corners of Everywhere.

Where does something like this begin?

It began with Shocking Crimes *and a simple connection. You then became I, and I have killed six women.*

He knew little about the Slave Murders and it would have stayed that way were it not for the special report on *Channel Two News.* Maybe he wouldn't have even watched it had Jana been there, but of course she was not.

"Residents of Bartok vividly recall the terror of twenty-five years ago when the murderer who called himself the Slave Killer stalked these very streets." The platinum blonde reporter, Geisha Hammond, gestured dramatically behind her to reveal the horror of Bartok pedestrians and middle class cars. "It was here in this peaceful community that the notorious serial killer took the lives of a confirmed four victims. Some experts believe the number could be as high as eighteen."

Cut to:

A so-called expert: Dr. Julius Vincent. "Why would he stop at four? This guy *liked* what he was doing. Nothing short of incarceration or illness would stop him."

Geisha Hammond returned. "Was the Slave Killer imprisoned for an unrelated crime or possibly committed to a mental institution? These questions cannot be answered definitively now, but one thing *is* for sure: After twenty-five years, some believe the Slave Killer has picked up where he left off."

That got his attention.

They played familiar news footage from the year before. Forensic experts and detectives got in each other's way as they scoured an open field. Like the point of a painting from which all lines emanate, a crumpled form lay behind them under a white sheet which fluttered in the autumn wind.

"The body of Deborah Willis was discovered on October 15th," Geisha narrated. "No one could know that it was only the beginning of a reign of terror." News footage from an almost identical crime scene intervened. "When Leslie Kinderman turned up under similar circumstances on November 17th, however, it began to seem chillingly familiar to long-time residents of Bartok."

The crisp picture of Leslie Kinderman's discovery became a more washed out, shaky clip from twenty-five years ago. More cops converging on an outdoor crime scene, with thicker hairstyles and cheaper looking suits. Disco Inferno after the body clean-up.

"The death of Anita Banks was a far more puzzling crime then, seemingly without any kind of motive. The perpetrator was thought to be a drifter, but the murder of Helen Mitchell a mere month later complicated this theory. The victims had little in common, except that they both caught the eye of a dangerous killer."

JOURNAL ENTRY, FEBRUARY 1

They were all whores. There's no story if the papers come right out and say it, because no one cares if some slut winds up dead in a ditch somewhere. So they try to portray them as responsible citizens. They paid their taxes, they provided for their children, they filled up soup bowls so a bunch of worthless bums wouldn't starve to death, etc.

If only everyone could see them the way I do, though. If they could hear the things I do when I notice them. Thoughts loud enough to be voices.

"That gleam in her eye—naked sexual lust. Something for you to see, but never experience. That's her game. Maybe you should follow her and teach her your game."

Maybe I should indeed.

He always found it strange and somewhat desensitizing when commercials interrupted something like the special on the Slave Killer. It created a subtext along the lines of "the murders of Deborah Willis, Leslie Kinderman, and Megan Ballard are brought to you by General Motors and Burger King—Home of the Whopper." It made it all seem like it was only a TV show; an eighteen-minute sitcom minus the canned laughter. This week's episode: Janet Lynn decides to hitchhike on Highway 88 and gets picked up by a bloodthirsty killer, who has more in his pants for her than just a butcher knife.

Channel Two News returned.

"But how did the Slave Killer come to be known by his chilling moniker?" Geisha Hammond asked viewers.

So-called expert Dr. Julius Vincent made another appearance. "He chose the name himself in the first of his many letters to the local newspaper, the *Bartok Daily*."

Cut to:

The first letter, as the camera slowly panned across each word while a narrator tried to affect the murderer's clinical lack of emotion (he succeeded only in sounding bored). A disclaimer appeared at the bottom of the screen: DRAMATIZATION.

Much like car commercials, he thought.

"I am the murderer of certain young women who keep turning up in ditches, fields, and drain pipes. These are fitting places for them, don't you agree? I stashed the scum where they wouldn't bother anyone, and now they're waiting to serve me when I leave this world. I would appreciate it if you would refer to me as the Slave Killer from now on, because that is what I am."

His body became aware of it before his mind. His mouth hung open and his heart hammered rapidly against the walls of his chest.

That writing . . .

He knew that writing. No, it wasn't because it belonged to the Slave Killer. He'd heard of the crimes before, of course, but he'd never seen the letters. He'd never read Dr. Julian Vincent's book, *On the Trail of the Slave Killer.* Ordinary citizens didn't go looking into things like that, he knew. No, he'd seen the writing somewhere else.

He grabbed a stack of Christmas cards he'd saved over the years and looked at the handwriting on each of them. The banal narration continued on the TV and he looked at the screen to compare as he flipped through the envelopes. He found the right one on the fourth try.

It was from his father.

JOURNAL ENTRY, MAY 3

I call it My Precious, like in those books about the ring. But My Precious is not a ring. Mine looks like a blind creature of metal, with very sharp teeth. To even put my thumb against it is to create one of those "cut here" dotted lines in my skin. That is the worst of its offenses against me, and I know of several women who probably wish they could say the same. We'll never know.

At night I keep My Precious in the nightstand beside the bed. My wife will sometimes want me to "make a woman of her," and I have to have it there. I have to know that at any moment I could reach into the drawer and take it out. When I stroke the handle on the nightstand, my wife becomes a woman. Those others, though . . . they were already women. I made them far less than that, not even recognizable as someone who ever might have been human.

"Well, isn't this a surprise," his father said. "Come on in."

He hadn't been here in months, even though they both lived in Bartok. He had his own life, and not one he thought really intersected with his father's. They had even less to talk about since the cancer found his mother four years ago.

"How's Jana?"

"About the same," he replied neutrally, taking off his coat.

"I've been meaning to get back since Christmas," his father said. "Somehow it hasn't worked out that way."

"I know how that goes."

"Grab a seat." His father settled into his favorite armchair. A talk show rerun played on the TV, the volume muted.

"How've you been holding up, Dad?"

"Ah. Can't complain."

He sighed. "Okay, we can stop with the pleasantries. I'll tell you right upfront, I'm here for a reason. Two reasons, really."

His father said nothing, just looked at him expectantly.

"You asked about Jana. Here's the thing. She's been gone a lot. All hours of the day and night, she's at meetings or working overtime for her clients. That's what she *says*, anyway." He paused.

"You don't think she's actually at work?" his father asked.

"I know she's not. I followed her last week. She could have made a fortune selling matchbooks if she'd taken about fifty from each hotel." He laughed without humor. "I don't know who it is. Maybe there's more than one. I don't even care."

"If you get photographic evidence that she's unfaithful, you can burn her ass in a divorce," his dad informed him. "I saw it on Court TV."

"I don't *want* to burn her ass in a divorce. That's why I'm here."

That classic fatherly look of confusion. "I'm not following."

"I know who you are, Dad. I recognized your handwriting on the Slave Killer's letters. You murdered all those women. I don't know how many for sure. It could have been four. Julian Vincent thinks you did eighteen. That's not important to me."

The look on his father's face must have been the equal of his own last night when he saw the handwriting—the dawning revelation. The pieces falling into place.

"They think you're doing it again, though—" he continued.

"I didn't kill those—" his father tried to interrupt.

"I don't care about that either. These dead women of the past year or two or however long it's been happening, they're all random. They're like needles being dropped into a stack. If you drop in one more needle, no one's going to notice. Not as long as it seems completely random."

His father was silent.

"Why did you stop before?" he asked. "Their theories are all wrong. You didn't die. You weren't imprisoned for another crime. You didn't relocate. You didn't get sick. But you stopped anyway."

JOURNAL ENTRY, JUNE 6

I must become you again. I enjoy what I do, but you can't continue the game forever. You have to appreciate the possibility, however remote, that they'll find you. Do you remember the unremarkable endings of all those Shocking Crimes *articles? Of course you do. You could almost recite them from memory, you reread them so often. How did it feel when the fantasy was stripped away to reveal the rather banal truth? The seemingly invincible phantoms were mere flesh and blood. Loners, outcasts, and petty criminals. They were nobodies once the chain of evidence led back to their halfway houses and shoddy apartments. The elaborate fantasy was simply dissected and filed away.*

It was like The Wizard of Oz. *Look behind the curtain and there is the architect of something that seemed so substantial, but no longer does, because there's just a little man back there.*

If they never get to see behind the curtain, though . . .

"I'm going to a bachelor party Thursday night at the Electra Complex. It's for a colleague. Lots of people will see me. If you do it then, they might still suspect me, but they'll know I couldn't have actually killed her myself. There's nothing to tie either of us to it, especially when they figure out she probably spent her last night taking it up the ass in a cheap motel. They'll throw it in with the latest batch of serial killings. Even if they don't, they'll probably be more interested in who she was having an affair with. You have to watch out for those jealous lovers, you know."

"And if I say no?" his father asked. The old man seemed rather cavalier about being discovered, like he'd merely been accused of lighting a bag of shit on somebody's doorstep back in 1983. *We always thought it was you . . . you were such a little rapscallion in those days! Ennis had to throw his house shoes in the gosh darn trash!*

"That's obvious, isn't it? I'll go to the police with what I know. I don't want to do it that way. There's no reason for it, even if you're still out there doing your thing. That's your business."

"I told you I wasn't. You do realize it's illegal to blackmail someone into killing your wife, don't you?"

"Yes. It's your word against mine, though, isn't it? You'll still go to jail anyway. You'll get to look forward to dying in a prison cell. Is that what you want?"

"I'm just saying that killing her seems a bit extreme."

He laughed again. "Look who's talking."

"Son, I'm almost in my seventies. Most people don't even want me on the road, and you're asking me to commit the perfect murder?"

"Not a perfect murder. She's the perfect victim, according to you. *'From now on, you'll never know if I'm the one who butchered these hogs. All over the world, there are others like me. Our number grows every day, and soon there will be fewer and fewer of the whorish scum you call your wives and daughters on the streets, and more and more of them stuffed down drain pipes.'* You wrote those words, page 46 of Dr. Vincent's book. I turned up a lot of other interesting similarities between you and the police profile of the Slave Killer, incidentally. Probably married, children. Some kind of security job because you weren't good enough to be a real cop."

"You watch that," his father warned.

"The point is, you want 'whorish scum.' Well, she'll be in my house Thursday night, practically gift-wrapped for you. Jana never misses her favorite show, even if she couldn't ask for a better opportunity to go slutting around. Should have learned to program the VCR, right? It will still be early enough after the show for her to go out. You know how these 'emergency staff meetings' are." He held up his fingers to create sarcastic quotation marks. "Follow her and take her when the opportunity presents itself. If she doesn't leave, you'll have no problem getting in. I brought you a spare key. I'll take her car somewhere more appropriate and they won't even know she vanished at the house. So you know what you have to do. Otherwise, I guarantee the police will be interested in your activities from twenty-five years ago, not to mention the past year and a half. It'll be pretty hard for an old man who never leaves the house to come up with a good alibi on the nights in question."

His father was silent for almost a minute, and then said, "Thursday?"

JOURNAL ENTRY: JULY 17 - JULY 22

(PAGES TORN OUT)

Jana was still there when he got home Thursday night. Most of her, anyway. For a moment, he thought he'd accidentally wandered into a slaughterhouse. He'd seen its like before, but never in such a refined setting as his own house. The kitchen looked like one of those avant garde paintings where the artist slings paint in all directions across the canvas, except this was apparently the work of a starving artist with only deep red on the palette. The bitter reek of sticky blood and lingering death clogged up his nostrils, heavy and sickening.

"You left out a few important points of your plan," his father said from the living room doorway. Dr. Vincent was right—evidently the Slave Killer brought a change of clothes with him to avoid leaving a crime scene splattered with blood. He was clean in spite of the carnage all around. He had a gun.

"Like the part where you tell the police your wife was supposed to meet me the night she disappeared," his father continued. "I'm guessing you were going to leave her car somewhere near my house. It sure wouldn't look good for me when the police showed up, especially when you suddenly noticed an eerie similarity between my handwriting and the Slave Killer's. Those were your exact words in your journal, weren't they? *'Eerie similarity?'* Then it would be your word against mine, and they'd probably believe you. They wouldn't know that the Slave Killer has nothing to do with the new killings. They have a profile of you, too, you know. They think you take out your rage for one woman against others because you're too damned chickenshit to kill the source. That's why you had to get me to do Jana; to 'share needles.'" He mimicked the sarcastic quotation marks with his free hand.

"You also thought there was a good chance I'd take the fall for this business you've been getting up to with all these girls. You thought you could stop cold with Jana out of the way, and get away with all the ones you've done. You knew she'd been cheating on you for a lot longer than a week. That's when it started for you. This all made for fascinating reading, though for the sake of dramatic license, I had to take any page that mentioned me in your plan. It's funny. All this time, and I didn't know my old issues of *Shocking Crimes* were the fuel for all your little wet dreams."

He stood rooted to the spot. Like his father earlier this week, he denied nothing. Dad saw the journal. It was all in there. "Where's Jana?" he finally asked, noting that while the kitchen was awash with blood so thick in some places he could see his own reflection, he saw no body.

"She's in the bedroom. And the bathroom. And the linen closet. She's on some of the stairs, too, I think. She's the one who found your journal, by the way. She was fretting over what to do about it when I showed up. I didn't need your spare key. I'm her father-in-law; of course she was going to let me in. She didn't even get to the best part about how her husband hoped to drop her in the stack with the rest of the needles. I did, though. I'm bad about that—I have to flip to the end of a mystery to find out who did it."

"I was at the Electra Complex," he replied calmly. "I nearly got into a fight with some guy because I almost knocked his beer over. He told me to watch what the fuck I was doing and called me a 'dicksucker.' A bunch of people saw this. They say he has a habit of getting in people's faces over nothing. They'll remember me. What happens when the time of her death doesn't fit in with when I could have killed her? Think about it."

It was his father's turn to laugh. "They've got a written confession for eight murders in your journal, and you think they're going to let a little discrepancy like that bother them? I even used your knife on her. Found it right where it was supposed to be. Your Precious."

"Look, Dad," he said, almost smiling, "I swear . . . it'll never happen again."

"No," his father said. "It won't."

Channel Two News—Special Report on the Bartok Butcher
"How did he sound when he called you that night?" Geisha Hammond asked.

"He was hysterical. He didn't say anything about what he'd done to Jana, but he said there was blood everywhere. He asked me to come over right away."

"And what happened when you arrived? What did you see?"

"He opened the door, and he was just covered in blood. Like he'd been *wallowing* in it. That's what I remember thinking when I saw him . . . *He looks like he's been wallowing in blood.* And that's when he started raving about all the other murders he'd done. I could see . . . I could see . . . Jana . . . I'm sorry."

"It's okay, sir. You take just as long as you need."

"Thank you. Uh, okay, so I walked inside and I saw what he was talking about . . . blood *everywhere*. He *destroyed* that poor, sweet girl who never harmed a soul. I took my gun because of what he said about all the blood. I was scared . . . wouldn't take any chances. I told him, I said, 'Son, we have to go to the police.' But he wouldn't hear it. He was like a mad dog, and when that happens . . . you gotta put them down."

The old man being interviewed wiped his eyes and repeated, "You gotta put them down."

"And does it bother you that people consider you a hero for what you did? At the cost of the life of your own son . . . your only son?"

"Of course it bothers me . . . they couldn't ever know the burden. And they *shouldn't*. No one should. It's like they say—the most tragic thing in the *world* is for a parent to outlive a child."

GENITAL GRINDER:
A SNUFF FILM IN FIVE ACTS

I.

"What's the worst thing you've ever done?"

"I won't tell you that, but I'll you the worst thing I'm *gonna* do . . . the most depraved thing."

"Does it have anything to do with this little movie we're going to make?"

Von only laughed. "I lied; I'm not going to tell you that either."

Greg smiled in return, and cast a backward glance to verify the cargo was still quite immobile. "All systems go," he reported.

They were eastbound on Gardner Drive, destination Von's house. They'd already run the risk of a hazardous houseguest in the form of Claire Perkins, the hit-and-run victim they'd kindly transported some time ago from Sherman Avenue (and Bowling Boulevard) to Von's for the express purpose of necrophiliac debauchery. Claire was currently cooling off in a crisper, at least what was left of her. After three days and nights of experimentation, they'd exhausted every nook and cranny. Von came up with an ingenious idea to dispose of the body, but it was slow-going. The entire feast would probably last nine days between the two of them.

Breakfast, lunch, and dinner—all Claire. If they'd known it was going to turn into this big a headache, they'd have just wined, dined, and married the bitch. He could scarcely believe at this point that he had been so thankful to find her before, but like anything new, all it took was a little over-exposure to remember that life had been just fine before her arrival. Nothing like blowing a few loads in a putrefying backdoor to rend the veil real quick-like.

No point holding it off any longer . . . it was about time for the *cunt a la mode* to add a little spice to the whole drudgery of the cannibalistic enterprise. He was actually looking forward to being back home for that.

But that wasn't the only reason, of course; there was the movie.

Hog-tied, gagged, and tarp-wrapped in the bed of his truck now was the infamous Sarah Pensie, better known to porn connoisseurs as "Lolita Ream," friend to the varsity football, basketball, and tennis teams back at Bartok North High School, not to mention the shop class and even—God save us—the chess club. Greg and Von hadn't participated in a damn thing, so they'd missed out. When they heard she'd gone on to a lucrative career in pornography, they'd *really* felt like Bill Buckner in game six of the '86 World Series. Down but not out, they decided to write to her. Against his better judgment, Von left the province of contact to Greg, a decision he'd dearly regretted when he saw what Greg evidently thought a "romantic overture." The gist of his letter, minus a broad interpretation of acceptable grammar:

Dear Sarah, we went to school together, but I never got to bone you in your sweet ass. I hate that you have missed out on this jizz rocket I'm strapping. All those guys in your movies look like they'd rather be smoking on a rope than giving you the hard yard, so do yourself a favor and get your ass back to Bartok for a real man. You won't regret it, baby. If you've ever wanted to be so pumped full of sauce that your eyes popped out of your head with your twat right behind 'em, I'm the man to see. I sent you some high dollar earrings last year, so I figure fair is fair.

Your pal, Greg.

P.S. Please hurry as the doctors tell me I may die of the sickle cell in a few weeks.

The bitch did not respond, however, necessitating this little road trip. Apparently too much time blowing Louisville slugger-sized hard-ons in hot tubs and doling out rim jobs aplenty had her thinking she was too good for all the "little people" these days. Well, maybe it was time for her to reconnect with her roots.

They'd staked out the P.O. box for her fan mail—and "gifts" that secret admirers could send her from her fan letter wish list, as if she wasn't raking in cash hand over quim with her videos selling for about 40 bones per. They watched the post office for three *very* uneventful and boring days and nights, passing the binoculars back and forth from a strip mall across the street. Even all the tight-shorted eye candy strutting it up the sidewalks grew a bit tiresome after they reluctantly made a pact not to get up to any "funny stuff" with any of them. They had to stay pure for Sarah and not endanger the mission. This rare display of restraint had given them plenty of time to brainstorm what they could do with her when they finally grabbed her. It was a blessing in disguise, because they'd come up with some solid gold indeed.

They'd actually almost missed her. She was totally slumming it in a jogging suit and sunglasses, but Greg recognized the swing of her ass (and the way she bleached that balloon knot, Greg could probably have picked it out of a police line-up) as she swayed through a door held open by an old man who not-so-surreptitiously scoped her backside as she floated past. She came out with a mail crate, probably filled with several envelopes, large mailers and boxes with some of the lingerie or high heels or other wish list items that some pathetic dick-jack believed would earn him some sexual payback puss (scraping together their nickels and dimes to order her a set of lah-di-dah earrings and only receiving some thank-you form letter with no instructions on when they should expect to meet her so she could spread her thighs and properly show her gratitude—they'd knifed the whole envelope open to verify there was nothing else in it—they knew only too well that it left a man with a hole in his wallet and a burning in his ass).

They tailed her to a supermarket and finally to her home, the kind of upper middle class pad owned by someone who ought to be able to buy their own damned earrings. They chloroformed her right there in her driveway as she popped the trunk for her grocery bags. They didn't think anyone saw it go down, but didn't linger long to find out. Von gunned it out of the neighborhood and backtracked to the interstate. Greg actually made a decent navigator. It was simple enough to find a vacant rest area (the kind of rip-off place where there weren't really any facilities and you had to piss between your open car doors if you didn't want anyone to glom your wang) and get her properly secured.

The sultry little slut was going to fuel quite the orgasmageddon, with her silicone-enhanced breasts defying the mere C-cup that stingy Mother Nature provided, forcing the game into double D overtime.

"Should've written back, slutcake," Greg yelled, though she probably couldn't hear him.

Truthfully it wouldn't have mattered if she did. She'd still be here now. She would soon have company, too, because Von and Greg had been quite busy when they weren't deducting on Claire Perkins.

What sparked the whole endeavor was a news report on the trial of Earl Newman, the alleged serial killer affectionately known as Mr. Drill Bit. He'd abducted eleven women and over the course of three days would subject each to repeated rapes and other assimilated degradations, and filmed the festivities on a camcorder. At the conclusion of three days, he attempted to lobotomize them with his namesake, to no avail. He gave up after four tries and settled for reducing their teeth to peppermint shards and spearing their eyeballs like fish until the sockets burst. This, Earl claimed, was the only way he could achieve orgasm (forgetting the videotapes showed an entirely different story). The strange thing was that he only filmed the rapes, never the killings. Snuff films, reported anchor newswoman Geisha Hammond, therefore remained an urban legend; an unverified crime.

Above the heads of Von and Greg, light bulbs appeared.

Naturally, the first to be abducted for the creation of the world's first sanctioned snuff film was Geisha Hammond herself. A stun-gun did the trick, and duct tape did the rest.

Trussed in the basement, not far from Claire Perkins' makeshift tomb, struggled Bill Glasscock, who up to this point thought his name was by far the worst card Fate had ever dealt him. He'd been at the park with his video camera under the pretense of filming a soccer game, though he was far more intrigued that the players of said game were 10-year-old girls. And if there was grass on the field, you could play ball.

He was rendered unconscious by a blow from a tire iron when he was returning to his car, too invigorated by the choice footage he had collected and the night of ball sack-draining soccer which awaited him back at his apartment. Von and Greg had taken precautions by getting him from Brackard's Point instead of Bartok; plus, they'd also needed a video camera.

For purely aesthetic reasons they took Travis Wicklund, who was handcuffed, gagged, and locked up in a coat closet. He sometimes told women on the Internet that he was an architect and other times an environmentalist. They got him walking home from his real place of work, the Burger King on Seymour Street.

Sarah, Geisha, Bill, and Travis. This was the cast of unknowns (well, minus "Lolita Ream" and maybe Geisha) who would involuntarily participate in the making of *Genital Grinder,* the first legitimate snuff film ever made.

II.

They chose a bathtub scene to open, because there wasn't a movie worth a damn that didn't have one. Geisha Hammond was more than happy to strip and get in the tub when Von brandished a machete. She was decidedly less comfortable in front of the camera than they expected for someone who made a living in front of it. Von decided it had something to do with the lack of a teleprompter, although the assurances that they would slit her throat if she didn't comply probably contributed at least marginally. She'd have to do without. Fortune had been smiling on them when it delivered Bill Glassock's Hi-8; they weren't going to conveniently catch a gentleman lugging a teleprompter away from a sporting event involving prepubescent girls. Geisha Hammond was wet dream material, so the bathtub assignment was a given. She always wore tight blouses with a little glimmer of cleavage, which made you feel pleasantly warm inside as you listened to an item about somebody blasted pointblank with a shotgun during a "drug deal gone bad" or a newborn tossed off a rooftop like a clay pigeon. Blond hair so light it was almost silver. Long skirts, but usually with a healthy slit up the side allowing a peak of bronze legs in the occasional fleeting long shot. And such lips . . . bee-stung and primed for pleasure. As she detailed the latest local atrocities—a single mother mutilated beyond recognition by the Bartok Butcher, a hobo pushed in front of a train, a cabin full of corpses by an old dirt track, a 12-year-old overdosing on heroin in an elementary school bathroom—all you could think was, *If she put those thick lips on my quim-splitter, I'd blast my payload right out the back of that blond head in about 2.2 seconds.*

Seeing her in all her nude glory now, he wondered why the hell he'd sat on his old beat-up recliner nursing a cold beer and a hard-on for the past few years when he could have just gone out and snatched her. All that wasted time. If his stomach wasn't lurching most disagreeably right now, he would have clamped his fingers around one of those solid ass cheeks (no tan lines . . . *none*) and expected a crack of lightning to explode through the ceiling and consecrate his hand forever as a sanctified object, holier than anything in the world of man.

The bush was only a little tuft of grass, allowing easy exposure of the other lips which could undoubtedly summon a skull-shattering payload in 2.2 seconds as well. It was all Von could do to stay back and not get in the way. He had to remember, they were here to create *art.*

"Just sit there and soap your titties," he instructed. "Improvise."

Genital Grinder

"Are you going to hurt me?" she asked. Her eyes couldn't seem to escape the hypnotic hold of the machete tapping against his leg.

"We can negotiate your contract later." He paused, his own eyes similarly locked on her legs, or more specifically *between* them, not exactly sure what he was seeing. Two yellow-greenish trails were rising to the surface of the water, like liquid worms. Others soon followed, creating a cloud, and a definite froth was congealing above her thighs.

Greg peered from around the viewfinder of the camera at this "breaking story" in Geisha Hammond's box. "Is that . . . cum?"

"You idiot," Von snapped. "You know women don't have orgasms." His stomach tensed again, although perhaps it had more to do with the Claire sandwich he'd wolfed down earlier.

"I have trichomoniasis," Geisha confessed, at first abashed and all miserable, but then her face brightened, suddenly hopeful. "I've only been on the antibiotic a couple days . . . and I missed the last dose because of you. Say, I'm not right for your movie at all—"

Von recalled a pamphlet he'd seen at the health department while waiting (and waiting . . . and waiting) to be seen. *You might have trichomoniasis if. . .* Even though he didn't have the symptoms described, it had spooked him. Each disease pamphlet he looked at seemed like an inevitable prophecy rather than something informative. Thank God he'd only turned out to have genital warts. No cure for that, so same deal as a broken toe . . . tape it and wait until you feel ready to get back in the game. He remembered from the pamphlet that over seven million people were affected with the disease. It was just his and Greg's sorry luck that they found one of them. What were the odds?

"Get rid of it," Von said. "It's spoiling the shot."

Greg looked at the mini cyclone of vaginal froth taking shape above her thighs. "Uncooked meat can do *that* to you?" he asked, incredulous.

Geisha flipped a hand through the water as though trying

39

to disperse a cloud of gnats. The froth merely expanded.

"Look, this just isn't a good idea," Geisha said, sounding as if she sure was sorry about this turn of events. "Why don't you just let me go? I don't want to ruin your movie, and I haven't had a good look at your faces anyway . . . I lost my contacts on the ride over here. I swear I won't tell a soul about any of this, okay? What do you say, guys?"

Von and Greg exchanged a look, and Von glowered back down at her. "I say, *get rid of that stuff.*"

"I can't," she reasoned, speaking slowly, as though her argument would get through to them if they just meditated on every word. "You want it . . . I want it . . . but it's just not meant to be. I'm not the right person for this movie. We gave it a good try, didn't we? Look, I'm a good sport . . . I'll jerk both of you off before I go."

"You'll jerk us off?" Von repeated.

"Well, yeah, of course!" She smiled, a crooked gesture that seemed to be holding her whole face together against a building flood of tears. "You can . . . you can do it on my chest if you want. Yeah? And you can blindfold me and drop me off somewhere . . . anywhere . . . and we'll forget the whole thing happened."

"You'll jerk us off?" Greg said.

She gave a mock two-finger salute. "Scout's honor."

"At the same time?" Von asked.

"Uh . . . sure, I mean if you want. How does that sound?"

"It sounds a bit homo," Von said, at approximately the same time Greg said, "That would be great!" Greg acted like he was adjusting the camera, blushing.

"Yeah, like Von said . . . that sounds homo. Both of us at the same time. But we can do it on your chest, right? One after the other, I mean. We could start with me."

She wiped her eyes, the smile dead on her face but maintaining position. "Whatever you want."

"Think you could hold it like that microphone you talk into on the news?" Von asked. "Like you're at a crime scene and telling everybody what went down?"

She didn't speak, just nodded.

"Good . . . we'll give you the chance to do that. But first, you need to get rid of that stuff and soap your titties up."

There was a long silence. She wasn't smiling now. "I can't," she said, gesturing to the discharge like it was a sea otter covered in oil, and her without her best brush. "Don't you see?"

"Eat it," Von said.

"What?"

"Scoop it up in your hands and slurp it down. C'mon. Time's wasting. We've still got two other scenes to shoot today."

"Let's just drain the tub," she reasoned. "It won't happen again after that."

"Lady, what kind of shooting budget to you think we have? This camera isn't even ours."

"But—"

Von raised the machete overhead without warning and swung it down into the tub. Geisha Hammond jerked back out of harm's way as the blade struck somewhere between her knees, splashing whatever over the sides of the tub and across Von's jeans.

He pointed the tip of the machete at her face. "I guess all actors need to know their motivation. Well, yours is to live five more minutes by doing everything I tell you to do. So when I tell you to eat that nasty looking shit in the bathtub, you better eat that nasty looking *shit* in the bathtub, because I promise you, the next swing won't miss."

She bent forward so quickly with her hands cupped that Von had to grab her wrists until Greg confirmed that he had all the action framed through the viewfinder. Geisha made a bridge with her palms which managed to encompass the majority of the discolored concoction. Some of it slipped through the cracks in her hands and fingers, but there was enough consistency to the primary concern that it simply caught there in the cradle formed by her hands. She raised them to her face, her eyes knotted shut, and opened her mouth to receive. She gagged immediately, even as Von urged her to lick the mucus-like trails that hadn't gone down

41

with the remnant bath water. A conglomeration of bile and the yellowish dregs she had just forced herself to swallow spewed across the surface of the water. The sight of it just as quickly prompted another round of a rancid torrent from her lips, which Von at least momentarily did not associate with 2.2-second load-blowing action of skull-decimating potential. The gastric debris was determined to congeal and remain afloat, like ocean foam surrounding an island.

Geisha sat horrified, sucking air, knowing better than to try to get up. Enclosed in a festering pool of freshly regurgitated giblets, she resembled the main course in a cannibal stew.

"Holy Antichrist," Greg said. "If the camera adds thirty pounds, you just lost twenty-five of them."

Von sighed. "Looks like you already jerked us off. I guess we don't have a choice now. I'm really not looking forward to the water bill this month." He pushed down the lever to open the drain. They made Geisha stand under the showerhead for a few minutes until the vomit rinsed off of her and out of the tub altogether. They refilled the tub and finally got the primo footage they wanted of Geisha, and then it was time to bring lover boy on stage as shooting moved to the bedroom.

III.

Lover boy in this case was Bill Glasscock, who wasn't sure what horrified him more—the prospect of being executed by his captors, or having to slide his beef baton into the bitch from *Channel 2 News*. To most men, she was probably *Playboy* centerfold material, but she was at least 15 years too old for Bill's sensibilities. Her lips alone could probably engulf the head of his member like a Dum-Dums sucker. No thank you . . . at least not if you weren't fairly new to the practice of long division.

He decided Geisha was the lesser of two evils when Von put a .357 to his temple, although as it turned out, he probably should have just taken the bullet.

Von was setting the camera up on its tripod when Greg called for him to examine the now-naked Bill. Von didn't have to ask what had spooked Greg, it was immediately obvious—Bill Glasscock had pierced genitalia.

Geisha, nude and shivering on the bed, now showed more than professional interest.

"Hundreds of thousands of people in this world and we keep picking up the freaks," Greg said unhappily.

"Stop being such a child," Von said absently.

Bill, mishearing him, perked up a little. "Really? Where?"

Von nonchalantly pinched the ring with his thumb and index finger and yanked it out abruptly, as though trying to spare himself prolonged pain while removing a Band-Aid.

Bill dropped to the floor instantly, bright red blood pooling in his hands and through his fingers. He cried out once, ear-splittingly loud, before Von chopped him in the throat. He curled into fetal position on the floor.

"What a pussy," Greg chided. "He's not in any shape to mount that snatch now."

"You can have the honors," Von offered. The whole business with the bathtub had left a bad taste in his mouth which he didn't think he could immediately put aside, even for the good of their movie. He couldn't stop seeing the facts from the *First Indications* pamphlet on trichomoniasis, a constant stream of symptoms across his mind like the crawl at the bottom of ESPN. Besides, those lips would feel just as good when she was a cadaver. Maybe even better.

Greg looked over at Geisha, who started shivering again. "Won't I catch her … mononucleosis?"

Von considered sharing the likelihood of transmission with his oldest pal and co-director, but then he thought of that toilet brush he'd never gotten back from Greg. Hell with it. He did offer a little sage advice as a compromise, though: "When barbarians are at the gate, your best friend is the back door."

Greg frowned, then had an epiphany. He gave a thumbs-up. "Lock and load, Von."

They used the bed sheets to secure Geisha to the bed

face-down, and roped Bill to a chair. There was going to be a prelude to Geisha's big scene, and unfortunately for Bill it would be at his expense. They positioned the camera for a static shot to promote authenticity. "Who will survive, and what will be left of them?" Von asked, cackling. He and Greg were crouched in front of Bill, who renewed his pleas for mercy—apologizing for having a piercing, for stealing Brach's candy from the grocery store when he was a kid, for seducing his sister's best friend, for seducing his sister, and for being born in general.

"You sure you've got us all in the picture?" Von asked, looking back at the camera uncertainly. He didn't want them to miss a frame of this.

"No doubt about it, son."

"Then hand me the screwdriver, Greg," Von said.

Greg plucked one from an array of tools on the carpet and handed it to him.

"No . . . the one with the flat-head." Von accepted it, squeamishly took hold of Bill's whole member, and plunged the driver into Bill's urethra. At this point they decided it'd be wise to tape his mouth shut. Another jab to his Adam's apple silenced him long enough. His wrists were bleeding from the struggle to tear himself from the chair. There wasn't much blood from the screwdriver insert, so Von asked for the ball peen hammer, which Greg graciously provided him. The testicles reacted more accordingly as the hammer dropped, one strike to each more than enough to mash them to the chair and subsequently burst them in a flash of skim milk white and deep red, a concoction that might have greatly interested the Cadbury egg candy makers. A healthy portion of it streaked up Von's arm, causing Greg to get the giggles.

"Not a word," Von snapped. "Remember who's holding the hammer."

Greg somehow stifled himself. "And for the coup de la creme . . ."

Von announced. "Greg . . . cheese grater."

Scraping his knuckles on one several times had given Von this idea. Disappointed by the lack of cruor from the screwdriver, this seemed like a good supplement. Greg held the grip of the screwdriver to properly elongate Bill's organ, which had actually engorged from the insertion, futile as that now was. Von applied the grater to Bill's skin and began the scrubbing, like someone with OCD having to sponge dry a white Cadillac. He half-expected Bill's screams to burst through the tape. He watched, fascinated, as he both saw and felt the skin and erectile tissue tear away. Perhaps most mesmerizing of all was the sound, wet and somehow reluctant. The head took the most effort, as the rim of course jutted beyond the shaft. Von had to really put his elbows into it. Blood and skewered fragments of dick were siphoning through the holes and collecting at the bottom of the grater. A spreading pool of it dripped off the chair, spattering the plastic they'd laid out underneath the chair.

"Shit!" Greg cried out. "Watch it! You cut my fingers!"

Von tapped Bill a few times on the crown of his head with the ball peen until the steady *thocks* became less pronounced, and soon sounded almost coital. Once penetrated, the skull allowed mushroom-like clumps of brain to spill onto Bill's face and in his lap, where it mingled with the genital carnage. To the untrained eye, it would almost look like Bill somehow had a miscarriage.

As Von polished him off, Greg got ready for his love scene with Geisha. She'd turned away from Bill the instant they started trading screwdrivers, so she hadn't seen what happened to him, but she'd heard enough to nearly rip up the bedposts. The knot work on the sheets had held up, though, fortunately for the world of cinema. They decided to keep her face-down on the bed, as that would be more convenient for Greg.

"Do you got any Jergen's or something?" he asked. They'd let her dry off after the bathtub scene, and *dry* was the operative word here. "This could be pretty rough going."

Von detached the camera from the tripod and went over to the bed. "Sorry. These are the sacrifices you have to make for art."

Greg considered this sadly, but then smiled. "Nature will

provide." He pushed his left nostril shut with a finger, and exhaled through the right. A cupped palm was waiting to catch the stream of mucus, which he quickly lathered on his half-erect dick . . . it then sprang to full attention. Geisha, who'd heard the exchange and the snot rocket, began thrashing anew, but Greg was used to women trying to evade him in such a fashion. He eased inside in two seconds flat.

Von loosened her gag to get some screams on tape, because you couldn't decipher from her grimaces if she was in agony or rapture. This was hardly the kind of film where ambivalence would be acceptable. He did his best to keep her choicest body parts in frame while trying to exclude Greg's less savory appendages. When it came time for the surprise, he came around to the foot of the bed, always keeping her smooth, bronze body in the viewfinder. Greg had finished by then, grunting in a way Von found overly theatrical and then pulling away from her with a harsh sigh, as if he'd just set down a 400-pound barbell. Von began to question his very sanity as he immortalized every curve available to him in her prone position. He'd let Greg have dibs on *Geisha Hammond?* Just because of some grody-looking froth in the bathtub? He needed to be locked up where he could do no further harm to himself. Von held the camera in place until Greg could get his pants buckled and take it from him. Von retrieved the bolt cutters from the spread of tools in front of Bill Glasscock. This was a tricky shot, as they needed to make sure she couldn't move her legs and destroy the angle.

When they saw she wasn't going to cooperate, Greg filmed while Von regagged her and took a hacksaw to the backs of her legs. It pained him, these little sacrifices for art, but he decided that as long as she at least had her lips and thighs attached to the trunk of her body, he would get the utmost satisfaction from defiling her later. Greg eventually had to set up the tripod again and shove the saw from the left while Von pushed at the right. The jagged teeth found a rhythm and began grinding through the supple meat. The rich crimson sluiced from the incision deepening across her limbs in perfect symmetry. The bones were predictably resistant, but even they had to give way eventually with enough elbow grease. Von pulled the limbs away with a little effort, ripping through the last of the arteries, veins, and sinews. It was like the trick where the magician and his assistant sawed through the boxes and wheeled them apart, except there was only one box here and it had yet to make its own contribution to the menagerie. Blood jetted from the stumps unimpeded as Greg tossed the limbs aside for later. He quickly took a knife to one of her restraints, and then got on the bed and stood with a foot on either side of her. He got his hands underneath her arms, and lifted. It delighted him when he saw how the stumps blasted out the red stuff that much more aggressively when he nudged her sternum, setting her down face-up. He held her in place, dangling her off the edge of the bed so that Von would have easy access.

Von slid beneath Geisha's torso on his back, as though working under a car. He carefully poised the bolt cutters as renegade blood squirted on his hands, arms, and chest, and quickly snipped off the right labium majora, then the left. They dropped on his face and stuck there like wet leaves.

Greg purposely stepped on her abdomen as he came down from the bed. The stumps shot supremely one last time. She didn't struggle much now, even with one hand free. That lovely bronze skin had begun to look quite pallid. Von stuck the severed lips on his ear lobes for a minute. They clung precariously like a playing card to a forehead, then slipped onto his shoulders like flesh-colored petals. He scooped them up and hurled the labia at the wall over the head of the bed. One stuck; the other slid behind the headboard, leaving a glistening red trail. Von turned his bloody profile to the camera and waved. "Hi, Mom!"

IV.

Initially, Travis Wicklund had been rather apprehensive about his abduction, but the worm had most definitely turned. They wanted him to screw *Lolita Ream?* By God, where did he sign? If this was the sort of fate that awaited someone who took candy from strangers, more people would gladly be snatched off the streets. This was a life-long dream, minus the aching blow to the head and whole kidnapping scenario. He was so astonished by this turn of events that he didn't speculate on what nefarious plans Von and Greg had for him afterwards . . . in Travis's mind, there *was* no afterwards. No before, either. He could face an eternity of flipping burgers on the fryer with this kind of memory accessible to him. He was actually going to bang Lolita Ream, porn queen supreme, full of his ball sauce, and that was all that mattered to him.

. . . Until he saw the bucket of squirming maggots and the transparent tubing beside it.

"We're going for a lot of firsts here," Von explained, fresh from a shower. They'd moved shooting to the spare bedroom and taken care to clean themselves up so Travis wouldn't immediately be tipped off to the likelihood that his services would not be required if they were ever to make a sequel.

"We want to be the first to make a—" He paused, catching himself. "*Movie* . . . of this kind. We want to have a zombie spewing maggots on Sarah."

Travis cringed. "I have to put those in my *mouth*?"

Greg almost laughed.

"No," Von consoled. "Not in your mouth. That's the good news, in a manner of speaking."

Inevitably he had to be tied to a chair, too, once they told him the game plan. The truth was that Von and Greg had already had a few turns with Sarah on tape, so "forcible sexual congress" with her was pretty old hat by this point. They had Sarah really stretching—and spreading—her acting legs. Who hadn't seen her ready and willing for all comers a thousand times before? The more spontaneous— and unlikely—the situation, the more eagerly she wanted it. Sarah Pensie having sex and *not* liking it, well, that was like an actor totally vanishing into a role. This was the magnitude of Sean Penn as Spicoli in *Fast Times at Ridgemont High*— method acting on a whole new level. They wanted Travis to have a go at her now for the sake of aesthetics, but not at the cost of the boredom of their audience. How could they possibly alter the predictable course of events? Guy finds weeping woman gagged and tied in spare bedroom. Guy unscrupulously rejects Samaritan impulses and uses her for quick gratification. Guy shoots load on the closest fetishistic body part to his stud missile—those alabaster buns or those silicone mountains. Wow, the wheel like you've never seen it before, no doubt about it.

. . . Unless there was some way to throw the audience a curve on the formula.

Greg, after a few objections, finally consented to feeding the tube into Travis's urethra. Travis tried to make it a challenge, so Von smashed a beer bottle over his head and sent him to Wonderland again. He collected the shards for other uses as Greg enacted phase two. He plucked a single maggot from the bucket, and examined it before guiding it into the other side of the tube. It squirmed blindly, but aside from the movement it looked like something he'd have dug out of his nose in kindergarten. When it had advanced substantially in the tube he put his lips on it and exhaled.

Von looked up from his activities with Sarah and chuckled. "I always figured you'd give a world class blow."

Greg shot him the finger. "Hey, do you want to do this?"

"I wouldn't dream of ruining your time to shine."

Greg collected another maggot and repeated the process. It was amazing what you could do on a shoestring budget if you just used your imagination and left some meat out to spoil . . . say, when you couldn't quite fit the entirety of your hit and run conquest into the crisper.

When Travis at last awoke with the dull throbbing in his head somehow magnified, he was relieved to discover the tube had been removed. Something didn't feel right in his scrotal sac per se, but Lolita was waiting for him to deliver the goods, tied down supine to the bed and gagged, so it would just have to be a problem for another day. He had a suspicion that blowing up her box with enough spunk to fill a tube of toothpaste would probably do the trick anyway. He gingerly maneuvered his way to the bed, wondering why Lolita had to make this harder than it already was by fighting him. He wasn't the enemy. Did she not realize how many burgers he'd flipped just to save up the jack to buy her videos? These might not be the conditions he would have imagined such an encounter as this taking place, but he'd begun to feel entitled to it. Other than a shaved sack and half again as many inches, the boys in those movies didn't have anything he didn't, and probably hadn't paid forty dollars for a volume of *Gaping Anus,* to boot. There seemed to be a pool of blood spreading underneath her, but he paid it no mind. She looked a little pale compared to the movies, but maybe it was a trick of the lighting. He gave up looking at her face and closed his eyes, latching both of his hands onto her tits as though to keep from floating off into outer space. The euphoria was so intense that a UFO could have landed on top of the house and it wouldn't have registered with him.

Greg found a good angle with the camera.

"Remember," Von warned Travis. "Pull out when it's time."

And less than a minute later it *was* time, because all the girlfriends Travis boasted about on the Internet had something in common—none of them actually existed. Quoth he: "I can't hold it any longer!"

He pulled out and aimed for Lolita's chest like the dudes in pornos always did. The first couple cubic centimeters were normal, if somewhat hesitant; after that, they were anything but. It was like a squeeze bottle with only a smattering of butter remaining which expels, tapers, jets, halts, and finally sprays haphazardly everywhere but where you intended. It was remarkably similar in texture to potato salad. The maggots mostly dribbled off the end of his equipment, but the first couple actually shot an impressive distance as though propelled down a water slide and launched up the mounds of Lolita's breasts, writhing. Travis looked down in mute horror. The load had concluded, but one last maggot depended from his urethra, still squirming in the swollen orifice.

Travis yelped, and made pincers of his finger and thumb. He slid it out, groaning sickly. He pinched it too hard, cutting it in half, and flicked the pieces away. He turned away from the abominable sight and retched.

"Tell me you got that!" Von pleaded.

Greg gave the thumbs-up. "We got the whole thing . . . the money shot *and* him puking at the end like a total pussy!"

Von clapped him on the back. "Travis, you've been a real sport, my man, so we're going to let you do her again. And no maggots this time, either."

"The only catch is that you have to use her ass," Greg added.

"No way, man," Travis began. "I'm not—"

Von cocked the .357, and Travis reached for Sarah's hips to turn her over real quick-like.

"No," Von said. "Don't turn her over. Just hoist her up some."

Travis did, and closed his eyes. He could see where the blood was issuing from the plundered orifice, but he'd just ejaculated a clump of corpse-eaters, so no reason to get squeamish now. It took him a moment to re-harden, but you might say he was an old hand at masturbation marathons, and he was erect enough to go again.

He felt the gun at the base of his skull. "Keep going," Von said.

Travis didn't understand at first why Von would even bother telling him that—may as well tell him, *Keep breathing there, bucko*—until he felt searing pain across an inch of his dick.

. . . then another . . . and another . . . Each thrust opened another wound, what seemed like a thousand cuts concentrated in a horribly limited space. He could feel rivulets of blood coursing down his shaft, then dripping off his scrotum and down his thighs, spattering in dime-sized droplets on his feet. It was doubtful he would have noticed a UFO landing on the house at this moment, either.

"Faster," Von said simply. The gun cocked again and Travis complied, now screaming. They let him; no gags this time.

Greg made sure to get a close-up when Travis was at last

allowed to withdraw. He crumpled on the bed, his mutilated sex organ gleaming like a skinned rabbit and bearing a passing resemblance to same. For a brief instant Greg discerned a tiny shard of glass jutting from one of the lacerations, one of the fragments from the bottle slammed over Travis's head . . . then implanted within Sarah Pensie by Von. A nicked artery was blasting like an automated Super Soaker. Greg continued to film Sarah, because the intercourse had caused an exodus of some of the glass shards. Now runny tissue from within her digestive tract was slopping from her anus. He wasn't sure when exactly it happened, but she was no longer screaming behind the gag.

Von held a pillow in front of the gun and placed it over Travis's face. No point in prolonging his agony; that would just be excessive. He did wait a moment while Greg sauntered over into better position with the camera, then fired. A fan of red streaks and gray matter exploded above Travis's head and across the carpet, as though he'd just had an idea too amazing to be contained within his skull.

Greg tracked over the debris until he captured Von in the viewfinder, still crouched on the floor beside Travis, smoke curling from the crevice blasted into the pillow. Bloody feathers floated to rest on the linen, the motionless body, the carpet, like snowflakes in a paperweight.

"I guess that's a wrap," Von said.

And with that, *Genital Grinder* had concluded.

V.

The clean-up afterward was rigorous, and they made themselves complete it before they watched the movie; otherwise it might never get done. They'd stored Geisha's meaty legs in the crisper (and the rest of her in Von's bed), and even though children were starving in Africa, they incinerated the last of Claire's remains. Whoever's turn it was in the bathtub, they kept the camera in there with them just so the other wouldn't be tempted to try to preview their masterpiece in their absence.

While Greg waited for Von to get cleaned up in the bathroom, he watched the latest installment in his preferred series of backdoor-based pornography, *Gaping Anus.* Von, in turn, watched a menstruation epic called *Ragtime Girls,* with the irresistible tag line, "They come with no strings attached!"

And at long last, it was time to watch their magnum opus of film-making, the *Citizen Kane* of snuff movies. Greg, never shy about pointing out the obvious, was the first to comment as the TV presented no Geisha, no Sarah, no maggot orgasm, but instead a soccer game with girls who could have just as easily been mistaken for boys if not for their long hair: "Sonofabitch, Von . . . we never did hit record, did we?"

DEVELOPMENT

July 18, 2001

I've never kept a journal before, but there's too much going on now that I can't talk about with anyone else. I feel like I have to keep a record. I guess this is also a precaution, too.

I'm Alex. I'll be a senior at Bernardo High School in a couple weeks. Check the honor roll, I'm there. I'm on the yearbook staff, which is probably where I first got interested in cameras. Someone had to photograph the cheerleaders, and I thought I'd never looked more like "someone" before in my life. I turned out to be a someone with a real eye for low angles.

I also play on the tennis team, which I don't recommend if you're hoping to attract the opposite sex. I was lucky if my parents or my sister even came to the damn games, much less Katy Hindley.

I don't know where to begin exactly, but I guess I'll start with my job. I develop film at a store I won't name, because I'd hate to lose your business. Once you hear about the Binders, you probably won't want to bring your film to me.

I took the job to save up for a car. It only paid minimum wage, and when I first started, I had every intention of leaving when something better came along. I just expected lots of snapshots from birthday parties, weddings, and Disney World, but you wouldn't believe the pictures people drop off. I guess everyone thinks I wear a blindfold when I develop their film. I've seen some unbelievably hot slutcakes bare-assed naked or in bone-stiffening states of undress. We're talking lingerie, swimsuits, nightgowns, and half of one or the other. They pose for their boyfriends and husbands, who don't have sense enough to develop film themselves or learn how. I bet some of the pictures were sent to amateur photo contests in skinmags like *Gallery* and *Buxxxom*. Some had a good chance of winning, although I've had the misfortune to see many who could have soured a rapist's sex drive faster than a chemical castration.

I saved them in the Binders anyway.

I get some fetish pictures, too. There's a surprising number of guys who go around secretly taking pictures of women's feet. It became a game for me to see if I could guess who took what pictures, judging by the individual requirements. "Darrin McDonel," for instance, had to have open-toed sandals and toenails painted red. "Harold Bennett" was into red high heels and pallid skin. "Jamey Fiala" only photographed women in black high heels with those thin interlaced straps.

"John Futchins" was bolder. He went for those upskirt pictures you can see all over the Internet. I didn't realize so many women in Bernardo were into thongs (and thongs were into them).

I saved all these pictures in the Binders. It didn't matter if customers paid for doubles or not, some of their photos were duplicated and added to my Binder. It filled up fast. So did the second, and I'm running out of room on the third. Customers have to write their address on the film envelope, and halfway through the second binder I started keeping track of who submitted each picture. It was an impulse, you know? One of those things that you do without knowing exactly why. You suspect you could figure out why, but you're almost afraid to admit it to yourself.

Sometimes I visit their homes at night and look in the windows. Just anywhere a woman who posed for some of the pictures might live. I don't know why. I can see more in the pictures. But I do it anyway. Not often, just sometimes.

I've never been caught. I wish I knew the addresses for some of Futchin's upskirt subjects.

It's not always the women from these photographs I watch. Remember I mentioned Katy Hindley? I've known her since sixth grade. I've had a hard-on with her name on it for seven years now, which she has only experienced vicariously through her yearbook photos. She knows I exist, but I don't think she cares. The closest we've ever been was a lab group for biology. We dissected earthworms, dogfish sharks, and fetal pigs together, but strangely enough, she went to Homecoming with someone else in spite of our intimate bond. That's okay, though. If her blinds are agreeable, I have my own private "homecoming" with her on Elvin Avenue three or four times a week during the school year, and more in the summer. This has been going on much longer than the other nighttime visits.

But I was talking about the great pictures I see on the job. They're the reason I have to go to 1201 Hodson Avenue tomorrow. I'll explain it then . . . assuming I come back. Like I said, this is not just a record, it's a precaution.

July 19, 2001

Okay, remember how that killer in *Silence of the Lambs* was based on some crazy motherfuckers from real life? One was Ed Gein, who killed at least three women in Plainfield, Wisconsin. His hobbies included cannibalism, necrophilia, and fashioning furniture, bowls, masturbatory aids, and clothing accessories from dead women. Waste not, want not, right? Ed could have taught home economics and interior decorating.

The other inspiration was Gary Heidnik, who kept some prostitutes hostage in his cellar. They were played against each other as he systematically tortured and killed them. Just goes to show you can never tell what's going on in the homes around you.

Unless, of course, you develop their film.

The house on Hodson certainly didn't look like the kind

of place you'd find a lot of missing women chained up in the cellar, assuming there is a design intended to suggest this. It's a two-story the color of earth clay with blue shutters, entirely visible from the street except for a few maple trees in the way.

The mailman stops here six days a week, never realizing. The resident probably didn't have subscriptions to magazines like *Unwilling Sex Slaves, Torture Made Easy for the Suburban Serial Killer,* or *Middle Class Murder,* though.

I rang the doorbell. I'd thought about what to say all week, and this was the big moment at last. I heard footsteps and there was a long pause where I had time to think, *Shit, he's not going to answer and I have no idea what to do next.* But the door opened, and I got my first look at him. (After we develop the film, it's packaged and placed on an in-store rack where the customer can pick it up. I rarely see them unless they have questions or they need one-hour photo service.)

"Mr. Owens?"

He squinted in the light—a scrawny, skeletal man whose smile may have seemed pleasant to anyone who didn't know his secret life. I bet it was the last thing seen by several women the police didn't know about, and I doubted they'd describe it as "charming."

"Yes?" he asked. The picture of innocence. I could sense the gears turning in his head; he'd seen me before, even if I hadn't seen him. If it was at work, I generally pay little attention to the male customers anyway, especially when the females are parading around in shorts and halter-tops.

I had this elaborate story about a lost basset hound named Gloria, but I found myself saying, "You're the one who took Cassandra Bittaker."

If the police dropped that line on him, I don't think he would have reacted, but this was coming from some kid he vaguely remembered seeing before. He couldn't quite conceal his discomfort.

"Are you out of your mind?" he finally asked—which wasn't quite the same as denial.

Let me get back to you on that one, sir . . . because sometimes I really wonder.

"Cassandra Bittaker back in May," I said. "Jenny MacColl in June. Aurora Fenech and Mariangela Bouchet in July."

Owens' expression gradually changed as I named the young women who mysteriously vanished in the past four months. Initially he had the look of a claustrophobic man on an elevator where the doors don't seem to want to open, but by the time I got to "Aurora Fenech," he was positively beaming. Like I was describing his greatest accomplishments.

"You read the papers," he said. "So do I. I don't go door to door making wild accusations, though. Maybe you should stick to the funnies."

"Maybe I should call the police," I countered. "I think they'd be very interested in your basement. That's where you keep them, isn't it?"

The whole time, he kept that smile. Fight or flight was in his eyes, but the smile never faltered. It reminded me of all those pictures where the flash gave people red satanic eyes, but they smiled good-naturedly all the same.

Owens surreptitiously examined the street from right to left. I knew he was looking for potential witnesses to his next disappearing act, having realized that he wouldn't be having this conversation with me if I'd already called the police. A SWAT team would have smashed through every window and door of the house.

"I wrote about coming here in my journal," I lied. He didn't have to know that I hadn't actually gotten around to naming names or reasons. "I went from house to house on your block, too, asking about my lost dog. 'A basset hound, long ears, sleeps about twenty hours a day, answers to Gloria.' If I disappear, someone around here will remember me. It won't be long before they figure out my last visit was at your house."

Sounds convincing, doesn't it? Wish I'd thought of it BEFORE I went through with this, and actually did it.

He looked at me like he was trying to solve an equation,

and the wattage of the grin finally diminished.

"Not only that," I went on, "but you know who I am. And I have copies of your pictures. It was pretty ingenious of you to nab all those girls without being seen, but you need to bone up on common sense."

He didn't look pleased with that remark at all. "Just what exactly is it that you want?" he asked, his mouth now barely a line on his face.

"Show them to me," I said.

July 19 (later)

I'm back. Damn telephone. People calling to ask how my mom and I are doing, as if they really care. We oughtta have the thing disconnected.

Anyway, I GOT TO SEE THEM! It must have been how those astronauts felt at the moon landing. One small step for man, one giant leap for sexual sadism. You go in the house, through the den to the kitchen, and that's where the door to the basement is. I made Owens go first, because I didn't want him to a) push me down the stairs, b) lock me up down there with the women, or c) both. Not that "B" wasn't without its prospects, but I'd only accomplish half of my goals. More on that later.

So we went down there, and of course it's just like the pictures, for the most part. The basement walls are stone, and Owens has the shackles driven into them. You aren't breaking away from those unless you come from the planet Krypton. There were also some empty shackles for future acquisitions. And speaking of acquisitions, there, from left to right, were the pretty little schoolgirls and co-eds all in a row. Alphabetical order, too. I thought it was a coincidence, but he consciously lined them up that way. It seems like a pointless risk to me if he has to trade out shackles, but Owens is a bit weird.

The girls are chained with their arms overhead, which makes their breasts rise up. I sound like *Gray's Anatomy*, don't I? Their tits, then! I'd seen tons of pictures, but never in the flesh, never right in front of me. Not even when I was looking into houses, even after three steady years outside Katy Hindley's. My sister always locked her room and the bathroom, too. It was like this huge conspiracy to make sure I never got to see the good stuff, but I found a way around it, didn't I?

It was all on display! Four downy clefts, eight TITTIES, and four sets of ass. Hours and hours of fist-pumping action if you just happened to sit next to them during a study hall, but in a place like this where you can blur the line between daydream and reality, the possibilities were downright exhausting.

I HAD thought about being a "law-abiding citizen" and calling the police when I first saw the pictures. If anyone ever reads this, I want to go on record as saying I considered it. But when I weighed the pros and cons, doing the "right thing" seemed like a real cop-out. Think about it. Let's say I reported the pictures to the proper authorities and they stormed the house, saving the women and arresting Carl Owens. Would I even get so much as a thank-you card from three of those women? It's doubtful. After all the psychiatric treatment for their "ordeal" and their "post-traumatic stress disorder," they'd either go on with their lives and purposely leave any reminders of the experience way behind them, or they'd try to cash in on their "tribulations." The bottom line came down to "Will good ol' Alex get some ass in return for his heroic benevolence?" and the answer was always "Not bloody likely." What WHORES! Some gratitude, huh?

So yeah, I may look like the bad guy, but it was worth it for the steamy thirty seconds I spent with Jenny alone. I'd thought about doing this with her for some time. You've never seen such a struggle before in your life, either. I bet she didn't put up half the fight when Owens came to collect his just reward. All that squirming and whimpering, you'd think Helen Keller's mom set her down on a hot stove. I have to admit, if half those thirty seconds weren't spent restraining her gyrations so I could even get it in her, it would have been over that much faster. I made sure to get in a couple squeezes of her TITS after I blasted off in her, because I forgot to do it in all the excitement. Nice and firm, fit right in the palm of my hand.

I didn't even care that Owens was watching (and he looked at me distastefully, if you can believe that . . . what a hypocrite!). I should have been more worried that he'd try something, I guess, but I'd offered to develop film in his house, and having found out how close he came to discovery, he liked the sound of that.

I wonder exactly what he would have said if someone else developed his film and called him on the carpet. I suppose he could have said it was just a make believe thing, and hey, I swear they were all over 18! Nothin' weird here, good sir. If no one recognized the girls, he might have even skated on that, at least for awhile. The pressure cooker hadn't exploded just yet with no actual bodies. A lot of people figured the girls just ran away and were shooting up dope and sucking dicks—believe me, I've heard the ugliest theories—while the rest whispered that the Slave Killer guy from twenty-five years ago was back. *Geisha Hammond does that story about him in connection with the Bartok Butcher, and she just happens to disappear? And now four other girls? You think that's a coincidence?*

For the record, I *wish* Geisha Hammond was on display between Aurora Fenech and Jenny. Just my luck that she dropped off the face of the earth before Jenny disappeared. Have you seen the lips on that woman? You'd blast the back of her skull out instantaneously if she wrapped those things around your dong.

I'm sure it pained Carl to have to share the girls, but the guy was so spoiled anyway. He inherited the house from his mommy, didn't have to work for anything. I'm busting my ass for minimum wage, and he's out joyriding, chloroforming flawless college girls for an orgasmathon. Pretty unfair, if you ask me.

My hand's about to fall off from reliving this great experience . . . and I'm getting tired of writing, too. More tomorrow.

July 20, 2001

Oh, I said there were a couple differences from the pictures yesterday, didn't I? It turns out Mr. Holier-Than-Thou can't abide by the cost of feeding the girls, so he improvises. Chunks of flesh are now missing here and there from thighs and stomachs (*Gray's Anatomy* note: The buttocks were left intact, thankfully). The good news is that the girls don't have to worry about their stomachs eating themselves from malnutrition . . . the bad news is they're experiencing self-cannibalism from the outside.

That was hardly enough to sustain them and keep them from looking like refugees from Auschwitz, though. It turns out there was a FIFTH girl, but she wasn't local. Owens picked her up hitchhiking (they never learn, do they?). It probably got the whole thing started, such an opportunity falling into his lap. This is, in fact, how he figured out the high cost of living (as in keeping a sex slave alive), because he had to start buying for two. Then three, because he had to grab Cassandra Bittaker. Why do that if he can barely afford to keep one? Because he HAD to grab Cassandra Bittaker. Check back issues of the newspaper for her picture, and you'll understand immediately. After some soul-searching (and coming up empty), Owens gave the hitchhiker one more for the road, then slit her throat from ear to ear. A good strategy move, when you think about it—Cassandra Bittaker sees just how valuable she is from his perspective.

Frugal as he is, Owens didn't have a very big crisper. The fifth girl couldn't possibly fit. One hacksaw and three hours later, though, Owens did the impossible. Now he had plenty of meat to keep the livestock fed awhile. He's crafty, I'll give him that much. It couldn't last, though, especially when he kept bringing in more girls.

I made him swear not to carve on Jenny. I'll feed her myself, if need be.

Today I got the privilege of doing the carving for the others, though. A few strips from Aurora's arms. I whittled all the skin from Mariangela's toes (which contributed little, but the reaction was worth it). The soles of Cassandra's feet, to prevent visible scarring. That was something! Peeled off like the skin of a potato. More bones in the human foot than you'd think. We're going to need a new knife.

Did the deed with Cassandra and Mariangela today, savoring the coming fun with Jenny. Went off like gangbusters in Cassandra almost on contact, but held out for five glorious minutes with Mariangela. Still haven't managed a bee-jay because of the duct tape over all their mouths, which seems unnatural (my not getting a bee-jay, I mean, not the duct tape). The pictures in the paper of Mariangela showed some of the most pouty lips imaginable. Not Geisha Hammond worthy, but they promised a soft landing. Friends and family claimed she wasn't taken without a struggle, because she's a tough one. I take that to mean she'd bite a man off given half the chance. It sure wouldn't be worth it to take the chance of those teeth.

So we're gonna need pliers.

July 26, 2001

The political correctness of the papers is hilarious, and actually quite dangerous. Hilary Stiglitz is the fifth (known) disappearance in the past three months. Police do not want to attribute her vanishing to the same person or persons responsible for the first four, but they won't reveal why. "We have some leads we're working on," claimed Detective Keene.

No one will state the obvious: The bitch was too ugly to fit the pattern! Cassandra, Jenny, Aurora, and Mariangela were gorgeousness and gorgeosity. Hilary was what happened when you pissed in a test-tube. She was (and I do mean past tense) one of those overweight women whose pounds congregate in one area—in her case, the ass. It looked like someone threw a blanket over a monster truck tire.

You wouldn't insult your dog by feeding him the remains. Your basement-bound sex slaves, on the other hand . . .

You never know what might develop when you drop off

some film and leave your address.

And yeah, I admit it . . . I took "the plunge" in her, too. But Carl did it first. You take that kind of risk, it seems a crying shame not to get the most out of your effort.

July 28, 2001

I watched Katy through her window tonight. I thought she was going to undress, but the phone rang. I have to be completely silent during the summer, because she leaves her window up. Even the sound of a zipper might draw her attention, but that's part of the thrill.

The phone call was for her. A new boyfriend, apparently. That was rather depressing. I can't help thinking that if I was the one she was so happy to hear from, I wouldn't need a basement of women to satisfy me.

Loneliness is vastly underrated.

I did my thing anyway, quietly as possible. They were still going on when I left. Then I went to buy a pair of pliers before the store closed.

July 29, 2001

We're going through two and three rolls of film a day at Owens'. I develop film for less than six bucks an hour for six to eight hours, then I go to his house and do it for free for a couple more. The upside is that I am already halfway through Binder Number Six.

Stock tip: Buy as many shares of Vaseline as you can.

July 30, 2001

Owens is pissing me off.

Remember what I said about my goals? That's plural. Katy was at least the second reason I got involved in all of this. It's been my plan to bring her to Owens' from the beginning—or better yet, to have Owens bring her there himself. He's got a great track record, six for six all told. Katy has everything but a COME THROUGH MY WINDOW, ABDUCT ME AND RAPE ME sign on her house. It'd be nothing for him to do it.

But he won't.

"It's not the right time," he said.

"What are you waiting for, a full moon?" I shouted.

"It's just not the right time," he said again.

So I got to thinking. It'd be nothing for him to creep through Katy's window and take her. It wouldn't be anything for me, either, would it? This time we'll be collaborating on a chemistry project—I'll administer the chloroform, she'll succumb. Then I'll bring her back to Owens'.

Owens won't object, because Owens won't be around anymore. I'll get the hang of this kidnapping thing, and I won't need him. I can have ALL the women to myself, with no more of those disgusted looks when I do as I please with Jenny. At least not from him, anyway.

No more sloppy seconds, and I get the van AND the house. You couldn't ask for a better divorce.

July 31, 2001

I've never kept a journal before either. I guess you've heard about me, but we haven't been properly introduced. I'm Carl Owens. I picked up this nifty little journal from Alex.

You've probably figured out that I still have my harem.

I noticed that Alex didn't care to leave out the truth whenever it suited him. I DID recognize him when he first showed up on my doorstep—from the papers. He was Jenny MacColl's brother (and I do mean past tense). He forgot to mention that, didn't he? He sure didn't seem like the kind of guy to be ashamed of anything, but I guess you never really know some people. For example, I didn't know that he wanted to kill me and take over my congregation. Personally I was just getting sick of him, and I thought I'd take my chances with finding all the evidence he had against me. He was dead to the world whenever he got going with Jenny . . . only this time he stayed that way.

65

Ryan Harding

His mother isn't exactly my type, but it'll be good to have some meat on stand-by when they get done with Hilary Stiglitz. I think I'll hold onto this for awhile. Mrs. MacColl might be interested in reading it.

It just so happens that I have some empty shackles between Aurora Fenech and Jenny. I guess the time is right for Katy Hindley. Elvin Avenue, wasn't it?

EMISSARY

I.

Gabriel saw the dead man on his way home from the video store.

He'd been thinking about the shift at Movie Heaven as he drove. Carrie and Renee had both been there, the teen pregnancies waiting to happen. And what were they wearing on a sizzling August day? As little as the law allowed. Gabriel spent the five and a half hours playing pocket pool. The clock couldn't pass slowly enough to suit him on days like this. He fully expected them to show up in *Barely Legal* any day now.

A stack of porno movies clattered on the passenger seat. He was allowed to bring them home, but he'd waited for Renee to take someone to the tanning bed and Carrie to restock some new releases before he'd made his move. If he had any chance of going out with either of them—and the past three months had provided precious little hope of *that*—it wouldn't help his cause if they knew he was going home with *Lesbian Airline Stewardesses, Carol's Arse, Dildo Delirium,* and that perennial customer favorite, *Gaping Anus.*

It all made for a bitter obsession. Working with the hot little sirens transported him through a time wrap right back into high school, as if there were a worm hole at the check-out counter of Movie Heaven. It hadn't been long ago at all, so his memories of countless young things in skin-tight

67

skirts, halter tops, blouses tied at the mid-riff, shorts barely longer than their underwear, and open-toed sandals were vivid. He couldn't talk to them then; his tongue became like the knots in their blouses.

Who the hell am I kidding? he thought. *I can't talk to them now either!*

What ingenious things had he said to Carrie and Renee today? "Hi." "I'm going on break." "Could you hand me that?" "Well, see you tomorrow."

Yeah, a real mystery that he hadn't scored with either one of them or—as he always daydreamed—*both* of them yet. The irony was that he wasn't a bad looking guy at all. Kind face, cobalt eyes, fair hair—the typical angel blueprint. Did Carrie and Renee sense some kind of ugliness inside him? Sometimes it seemed like they must; them and all the beautiful ones he saw at work. He'd be happy just to get a sniff of even the middle tier women who frequented the tanning beds virtually every day that ended with a Y. Well, he could think of a thing or two he'd like to do at *their* Y's. They looked like they knew he was thinking this when he confirmed their tanning appointments . . . an uneasy disgust in their eyes with a tilt of the chin, like he had snot hanging from his nose. Even when he *wasn't* thinking anything untoward, he felt their derision. They sensed a strangeness, as if he had a pheromone that sent them all scattering instead of attracting a single one of them.

And there was indeed something Carrie and Renee wouldn't like if they knew about it: the *Taste of Death* movies. He was even more cautious about taking those home than the pornos. They might think he was pathetic if they knew about the pornos, but if they knew about *Taste of Death*, they'd think he was *psychotic*.

It was the *Taste of Death* series Gabriel was thinking about when he saw the dead man. He was standing on the corner of 37th and Garren, and to look at him you wouldn't know he'd had his head blown off on *Taste of Death 5: Into the Grave*.

These weren't simply movies where a group of horny

teenagers were slain with phallic implements. Like *Traces of Death, Faces of Death, Death Scenes, Executions,* and their brothers in the mondo video line, they were known as "shockumentaries." They provided the audience with various clips of real deaths caught on tape—accidents, murders, and animal attacks featured most prominently. Offended people erroneously called them "snuff movies," which differed in that a snuff victim was brought before the camera for the express purpose of being murdered. According to *Channel Two News* reporter Geisha Hammond (and the lips on *that* sizzling hot piece . . . Gabriel figured he'd blow the back of her head out approximately 1.5 seconds after she put those lush lips on his ramrod) in a story about "Mr. Drill Bit" Earl Newman just a few months ago, there was no evidence to support the claim that snuff movies existed anyway. Shockumentaries merely collected random atrocities where a camera just happened to grab the money shot.

One of Gabriel's favorites was a clip which showed a man blasted in the face with a shotgun fired off-screen. A moment after he blinked with the incomprehension of a bovine, his hapless look was erased in a shower of deep red and mushroom colored fragments, too many to count even in slow motion. Above the sounds of blood droplets and skull pieces wetting the pavement, an unnamed narrator cracked in Crypt Keeper throwback, "The world's foremost magician—now you see him, now you don't."

It was swift, senseless . . . a moment allegedly grabbed by a bored passenger tracking with a video camera at a traffic light. A graphic art born of nothing, never to be forgotten once seen. Gabriel certainly hadn't, and yet that same hapless gent now stood on the corner of 37th and Garren, unaware that his head had once been liquefied into a Sistine Chapel of Rorschach artistry. That wasn't the kind of thing you could fix with a tube of superglue and infinite patience; there wasn't supposed to be any sequel for you on *Taste of Death.*

The company who released the videos—Chosen Few Pictures—had clearly swindled him. He'd never suspected otherwise, even though some of the other mondo films were faked. He'd blindly trusted this series because it appeared to deliver what it promised in bloody red letters on every box: COMPLETELY AUTHENTIC! ONE HUNDRED PERCENT REAL! ARE YOU SURE YOU CAN TAKE IT?? (Funny, but he'd swear he'd rented pornos with an almost identical tag line.)

Not so. The shotgun decapitation only *looked* genuine. Unless the man was a ghost. A phantom condemned to walk the earth for failing to avoid what had to be a rather obvious murder.

Gabriel blinked, and looked for the man again. He was gone, now obstructed by the buildings on Garren.

Whatever the explanation, Gabriel felt disturbed. He'd seen each *Taste of Death* at least three times. The new one, the ninth installment, was due out next week. He'd been looking forward to another ninety minute foray into the final, intimate misfortunes of strangers. But it was for naught. That age-old certainty of death wasn't even for sure anymore.

He drove home to his parents' house, still wondering.

II.

The next day, he picked up each of the *Taste of Death* boxes and searched them.

They all listed Chosen Few Pictures as their distributor, but none of them gave an address for the company. As far as he knew, this was the only line of videos they had ever released. They had nothing else available for order when he searched the computer at work.

It had begun to dawn on him how strange it was that he had seen one of the "actors" from *Taste of Death*. He hadn't recognized the scenery in the movies, so it didn't seem possible they had been filmed in his hometown of Bartok. Of all the places in the world, it was quite a coincidence that he'd seen the actor here.

He started to question if it was a coincidence after

all. The chances of the guy having a twin brother seemed even more remote. Even in the scantily-clad company of Carrie and Renee he had difficulty thinking of anything other than what he'd seen the night before. His thoughts hadn't been this concentrated since he'd first brought home a *Taste of Death* movie, on a whim. The ways the people lost their lives, the strangeness that someone happened to be there with a camera, and just knowing there were even more of these shockumentaries out there . . . it obsessed him. Would his own death end up on a movie? Years of being alive, having friends, making an impact—however slight—would it all be eclipsed by a bizarre equation resulting in Gabriel Reynolds dying on *Taste of Death 10, 11, 12,* or whatever? Would he stop being Gabriel Reynolds and become "that dude who got snuffed on candid camera?"

The shockumentaries were a paradox. Even when you were certain that what you were seeing was genuine, it was still a concept that could not quite be grasped. How could these people you were seeing for the first time already be dead? Their deaths seemed real, but *they* didn't.

He ran a search on the Internet for Chosen Few Pictures. Thankfully it wasn't one of those names that would return hundreds of thousands of results. He found what he wanted right away—an official homepage for the company that had only recently gone online. It didn't tell him much, aside from their past releases ($39.99 per . . . thank God he could cherry pick the damn things when overstock wound up in the "previously viewed" sale bin) and the announcement that the new *Taste of Death* would be out August 6th (it had been pushed back, though, according to the Movie Heaven release schedule, and wouldn't be out until August 20th). It did, however, give him the contact address.

Chosen Few Pictures was run out of a post office box in Bartok.

III.

Not all of the clips could have been made in Bartok, though; Gabriel would have heard about it. For instance, *Taste of Death 3* featured a burning skyscraper where several people chose to plunge to a messy death rather than burn alive. There were no skyscrapers in Bartok; the clip had to come from elsewhere. It was probably true of most.

The common way to accumulate all this footage was to take out an ad in *Variety* or some other movie trade magazine and request news stations, police departments, departments of transportation, and the like submit videos with violent footage to the address.

Did this mean a few deaths were faked in Bartok for supplemental footage? The series was good about not borrowing from other shockumentaries. Maybe the only way to reach ninety minutes without resorting to recycling footage was to create new scenes. It made sense, and it was hardly the first time a video was guilty of false advertising.

Gabriel thought it was somehow unnatural that Chosen Few Pictures was run in his city, but of course it had to be *somewhere*. It could have just as easily been some other skyscraper-less city with a horny video store clerk who thought it almost conspiratorially bizarre that a mondo video company would have its home base there. He became less apprehensive about the coincidences, but was more curious than ever to see how the next installment turned out.

IV.

On August 20th, he got his chance. *Taste of Death 9: Grave Matters* came out with no further delays. He took it home that night. Its plastic box seemed to radiate energy, something that promised his eagerness would be rewarded. He watched it slide around on the passenger seat as he drove, as if it would accidentally slip and reveal its true self.

The cover had been decorated with an autopsy table and a stainless steel tray featuring the tools of dissection.

The back of the box warned of the violent content within, promising the death clips of a man who should have paid more attention to a DON'T FEED THE BEARS sign, movie stunts gone horribly awry, results of drunk driving on the Autobahn, alligator farm mishaps, PCP addicts in shoot-outs with the police, the final escape attempt of famed magician Isaac the Invincible, riots, tightrope walkers who laughed at safety nets, and assorted other punishments for hubris and just being in the wrong place at the right time. It promised to be the best shockumentary yet, a veritable extravaganza of morbid atrocities.

It sounded like just what the doctor ordered after an unproductive five hours of half-hearted banter that left no impressions on Carrie and Renee, or at least not any good ones.

He nuked himself a TV dinner, took it to his room, and parked in front of the screen. He was especially on the lookout for any possible Bartokians and local settings. As it turned out, they were more obvious than he would have believed.

"This young woman should have just called Triple-A," the narrator opined, with the assurance of one who knows he has just gotten off a sterling quip. The scene was purportedly captured by a nearby security camera. The female in question was leaning underneath her car hood in an otherwise empty parking lot, hands constantly fidgeting to signal she had no idea what she was doing. The scene occurred at night and was somewhat obscured by shadows. Another figure, probably male, appeared beside the woman, his face a silhouette. He seized the car hood and repeatedly brought it down across her back and head, instantly bringing her to her knees. The killer stepped back to admire his handiwork, his face still cloaked by the night. Without the overdone shadow work, Gabriel would still have been able to assess the authenticity—or lack thereof—in this scene. Though her tormentor had remained hidden by the unrealistic lighting scheme, the victim herself had not.

It was Carrie, whom he'd been admiring at Movie Heaven a mere two hours ago.

V.

"I didn't know you wanted to be an actress," Gabriel said to her the next day.

"I didn't know I did either," Carrie replied smartly, rolling her eyes for Renee's benefit. Renee giggled in that shrill fashion that always made her a distant 2nd to Carrie in his private list of Hottest Movie Heaven Trim. When his attempts at mirth with them inevitably failed, her refusal to laugh became a silver lining unto itself.

He smiled bitterly at Carrie's predictably evasive response. Weren't they a class act? Hiding things from him, sharing their meaningful looks, whispering to each other off in the corner (which always resulted in Renee's ear splitting histrionics, like Carrie was Eddie Murphy or something, and of course Gabriel knew they were talking about him), playing their little games. How long had they been perpetuating the charade? *All along?*

"But I've seen your work," he announced when Renee's laughter blissfully ceased.

"What's he talking about?" Carrie asked Renee.

"I don't know . . . but I bet it's sexual harassment, whatever it is."

"On *Taste of Death 9*," Gabriel explained, with a calmness that really surprised him. He felt anything but, especially with Carrie talking about him like he wasn't there. He was already tossing around the idea of taking one of Movie Heaven's rental VCR's home so he could get a copy of Carrie's death, just for ha-ha's.

"*Taste of Death 9?*" She couldn't have looked more disgusted if a leper had tried to solicit her for oral sex.

"Yeah," Gabriel grinned. "You know, the one after eight, but before ten?"

Renee didn't laugh at that, he noticed.

"How can you watch that trash?" Carrie asked, her face all knotted up into almost a natural Renee Zellweger look. "That's really sick, Gabe."

"At least I didn't star in it." He turned to check out a

customer, a beady-eyed man who had selected an interesting variety of videos: *Dumb & Dumber, The Ten Commandments,* and *Gaping Anus.*

Gabriel felt compelled to comment on the last choice. "That one's four hours long."

The customer's lips split apart to reveal teeth stained by nicotine and coffee as he smiled. "Yeah . . . I know. "

By the time Gabriel had collected the man's money and warned him about his snowballing late fees (he had a feeling that the customer, Greg Bracken, probably wouldn't be getting these back on time either . . . four hours was quite a commitment), Carrie and Renee had deployed themselves to other parts of Movie Heaven, probably just trying to put some distance between him. He saw them huddled up over in comedy, inconspicuously standing in front of '80's sex comedies like *The Last American Virgin* and *The Joy of Sex.*

No hee-hawing this time, though. Worried. That was good. They had every reason to be.

VI.

At the stoplight at 37th and Garren, he had to crack the window—he felt like he was suffocating.

The shotgun fatality was back, and so were eight other people he had seen meet some very colorful ends on the latest Taste of Death. There was the blonde woman with the ponytail who got her throat torn out by a rabid dog ("Man's best friend, but not such a success with the ladies"). The guy with the crewcut who'd gone through his windshield after hitting a telephone poll ("He should have dialed 1-800-COLLECT"). Two of the promised PCP addicts who'd gone out in a blaze when surrounded by police, one screaming that he was Jesus Christ ("Somehow I don't think he'll get up in three days") and the other pleading for someone to "Get them off me!" And still others.

He punched the accelerator and drove through the red light, narrowly missing one of the angel dust addicts on the crosswalk and a car making a wild left onto Garren, not letting up on the gas until he was home.

He didn't get out of his car immediately. He sat there, his hand shaking, sweating bullets which had nothing to do with the August heat.

What in the hell was going on? He could accept that the shotgun man didn't really die; pack a prosthetic head with blood-filled condoms and blast it, the effect would be very similar to the real deal. But what about the others? The woman with the ponytail, for instance. The camera *never* left her as the dog burrowed into her throat. There had been no chance to cut away for a special effect. He'd watched the life vanish from her eyes, and he'd seen the torn remnants of her throat and shards of neck bone when someone finally got a lariat around the dog and hauled it away (someone unceremoniously shot it in the head, again with no cutaway).

She'd died, he had no doubts about it. Same with the PCP addicts, because wherever they'd had their last rush, it hadn't been anywhere in Bartok. If he lived anywhere else but here, he could rationalize this all as extremely realistic special effects.

Was he losing his mind? It would be the natural conclusion if he told anyone what he'd seen, and more importantly what he thought about it. His parents would have him committed to the Sunshine Elkins Institute over in Hasbrouck. There had been a guy from his high school who wound up at Elkins. A chronic masturbator. It may not have been such a problem, but any place became a good place for him to jack. The bus stop, the cafeteria, the bleachers at a pep rally, driver's ed (once as a backseat passenger when it wasn't his turn), and the straw that broke the camel's back, career day. A lot of parents and important visitors on hand that day . . . and he was on hand, too, right there during a presentation from a cop with a K-9 German shepherd who looked very puzzled by the whole display. An apoplectic PTA mom demanded the cop drag him off to the electric chair on the spot. The jokes about him had lasted until graduation, wondering what kind of business he could get up to with a whole graduation gown to hide the ol' slapstick. It didn't seem very funny to Gabriel now, though. He'd go insane if they locked him up . . . if he wasn't already.

He thought of Carrie and smashed his hand against the dashboard. She knew what was going on . . . she was in on this. It was some kind of game. Why else would she have such a flippant attitude when he confronted her?

He didn't get out of the car for quite some time.

VII.

Two things of interest happened the next day. Someone rented *Taste of Death 6: To the Gory End*. He wanted to open up to the guy about what he'd been seeing around town, but the girls had been right there, sharing a disapproving look when they noticed the title of the video. *Why don't you dumb twats go lez out in the tanning room?* he wanted to say, but the idea caught his fancy and he found himself embellishing the concept in his mind periodically for the next three hours. He never entirely forgot about the customer, though, and when he showed up later in the afternoon, Gabriel felt a rush of excitement.

He knows . . . he's seeing all the victims around town now, too. He has to see the ninth one now, with Carrie's big scene.

Renee was on her lunch break and Carrie was back in the bathroom. He couldn't have asked for a better opportunity. But it was nothing like that.

The customer struggled to find the adequate words. "Uh, yeah, I rented this, like ... earlier today?"

"I remember," Gabriel said. The lack of urgency (and articulation) immediately diminished his expectations. It couldn't possibly be what he had hoped. The guy would have practically walked through plate glass and barely noticed it if he'd really *seen*.

"Right, okay . . . uh, yeah, the tape is, like, blank and stuff."

"Blank?" Gabriel echoed.

"Yeah . . . and stuff? It's all, like, static."

And stuff. Yeah, I know.

He'd been switching them out for the weeks leading up to the release of part 9. They had all played just fine. Some had more tracking issues than others, but they all worked.

"Sorry about that . . . we'll see if we can fix it. Or do you want to exchange it for something else?"

The guy looked over his shoulder, and Gabriel briefly wondered if he thought he was being watched. Maybe this was all a charade to deflect suspicion.

Satisfied by what he saw, the customer turned around and quietly asked, "Is, uh, *Gaping Anus* back in stock?"

Gabriel sighed. "The new one, the 24th? No. Not yet."

"Twenty-three, then?" he asked hopefully.

Descending order of availability finally made it all right with volume number nineteen, if a bit begrudgingly (the 4-hour "butt banging bonanzas" didn't start until volume twenty, so "2-1/2 hours of butt stuffing madness" would have to suffice . . . and as obsessed as the customer seemed with the concept of "stuff," he couldn't have been too awfully disappointed). He also put himself on the reserve list for a Lolita Ream movie after confirming Gabriel's work schedule.

Much later, the idea of the blanked video cassette seemed ominous to Gabriel. Yeah, maybe the guy wanted *Gaping Anus* all along and just didn't want to bring it to the counter with Carrie and Renee standing around, although why not get something a little less off-putting if you're worried what some hot girls might think of your choice? Gabriel obviously wasn't going to test the movie out here at work, though. He took it home, unsurprised in the least to discover it played just fine, arguably with even less tracking interference than the volumes before and after it.

The other significant thing was that he went back to the Chosen Few Pictures webpage, and found a significant change.

Taste of Death 9 had been pushed back to August 27th. This update was made today, the 21st.

"But it already came out," Gabriel said, dumbfounded.

VIII.

It being Thursday, Gabriel, Renee, and Carrie were at Movie Heaven until 9:30 as the closing shift. Renee's mother picked her up just as the trio exited (she had not-so-politely declined a ride with him in the beginning, and he'd never offered again).

And then there were two, he thought.

He locked the doors to Movie Heaven, trying to hurry. He heard Carrie's rushed footsteps, her sandals thwacking on the asphalt as she hurried to her car.

Must be my winning personality.

The lock and keys fought him, and Carrie's car door was slamming shut even as he turned around. It enraged him, even though he knew she wouldn't be going very far. When her car flooded, she slammed a fist across her steering wheel.

He thrust his hands in his pockets and began shuffling over to his car, singing an old Doors song, "Strange Days," to himself. He threw a cursory glance around the lot. The other stores in the shopping center closed up at 9:00. There was just one other car in the lot besides Carrie's, and unfortunately for her it was his.

Her hood popped up, and Carrie reluctantly slid out of her car, looking at Gabriel out of the corner of her eye. He knew what was going to happen now; what *had* to happen.

"Don't start with me," she warned as he closed in. "Just please tell me you know something about cars."

"Naturally," he said. He couldn't so much as replenish windshield wiper fluid; that's what his dad was for. He smiled at Carrie disarmingly, idly wondering if the patron from yesterday really planned to watch *The Ten Commandments*.

Carrie adjusted the stand to keep the hood propped, thus eclipsing the extent of Gabriel's automotive know-how.

"Any idea what's wrong?" he asked, trying not to laugh.

"I wouldn't ask for your help if I did," she answered in singsong.

"Well, I'm a Samaritan. I'd have helped anyway." He leaned under the hood, feeling her spiteful look. He yanked something at random, and was rewarded when it slid out. "Hey, I might have found something. This thing here is loose." He held it up for her inspection.

Carrie sighed with a bonus eye roll, even though Renee wasn't around to enjoy it. "That *thing* tells how much oil is in the car." She snatched it away from him and guided it back into its proper place, mouthing a stream of obscenities which he gathered weren't in high praise of his character.

She hunched forward, brushing her fingers with her thumbs to wipe off grease. Gabriel enjoyed the rear view as he cracked his knuckles.

"You should have called Triple A," he said, too quietly for her to hear.

"Hey," Carrie said excitedly. "This wire isn't—"

He smashed the safety bar with the palm of his hand, dislodging it. The hood slumped down, striking Carrie across the back. It wasn't much, just enough to stun her. It was all he needed. He hoisted the hood up and slammed it back down, increasing his momentum by jumping. She sank to her knees. She made an effort to slide out of harm's way, but he blocked her off and reaped some well-earned frottage as he delivered six more compacting blows in rapid succession The last few came down on the back of her neck, eliciting tiny pops as vertebrae cracked.

As the script called for, Gabriel took a few steps back and observed the scene. Carrie was sprawled in front of the car now, arms jutting out like broken wings. Motionless.

Gabriel looked back at Movie Heaven. He thought he saw a red light in the darkness, like the one which glowed on his father's video camera when it recorded. He couldn't see clearly, but he didn't have to. The article in the paper this morning had told him what was going on, the simple headline reading BARTOK WOMAN KILLED IN RABID DOG ATTACK.

Seven simple words, all it took to make him see what was written . . . and what was prophesied.

IX.

The emissary of visions unclaimed found him again—the hapless individual at 37th and Garren. About to return to the wife and kids, maybe, or at least thinking he was. Not paying much attention to Gabriel, or the strange way he hunched over to obscure the shotgun as Gabriel stepped out of the car.

"Are you ready to do your magic?" he asked, approaching the man. He stopped five feet away from him.

And waited for him to blink.

GENITAL GRINDER II:
DIS-MEMBERED

Part 1: Genital Finder

The Electra Complex was a beacon for the lost souls who had nothing better to do on a Saturday night than have the same tits from last weekend thrust in their faces.

Some souls were more lost than others, which is where Von and Greg came in. They were no strangers to the nudie bar circuit. In a couple dives they were known well enough to elicit a greeting like Norm's from *Cheers*. The Electra Complex, however, was not one of them.

"I'm sure glad we ain't actually paying ten to get in," Greg said.

Von concurred. "I'm all for full nudity, but it ain't nothing I couldn't see from my own mother. And hell, it don't cost me near as much."

Greg seemed distressed by this. "You get some kind of discount being blood-related or something? I'm out an Abe Lincoln and a couple Washingtons every time."

Von laughed. "You're getting your ass burned, son. I was in it for nine months and it didn't cost me a dime. The milk was free after that, too. For awhile."

Greg was not Von's "son." It was merely a colloquialism they had cultivated over the years.

"Hell, though," Von continued, "it won't put you on welfare to spend ten to look at some titties now and again. Safer, too. Ma's retirement home is getting suspicious."

82

To sit here and complain about paying ten bucks to see naked women when they were going to be millionaires before the night was over was absurd. Every slut had a price, and they'd be able to afford it. They wouldn't have to slum anymore. There'd be no daring sieges on the dumpster behind the gynecological clinic, sifting for used sanitary napkins and sniffing the fingers of discarded rubber gloves. Finding out the clinic didn't properly dispose of hazardous waste was among the five luckiest things to ever to happen to them. Scoring above that landmark occasion was the miraculous rumor of a doctor's visit by a certain red-headed TV star who often investigated crimes with paranormal circumstances. Von and Greg kept every single pair of gloves and each blood-soaked tampon they found that night. They pored over them at least bi-weekly, wondering if this or that had come from within the gilded snatch. They'd wrung every last drop of juice form the tampons into a beer mug and traded swigs. The rumor had never been confirmed, but on still nights where a sudden breeze ruffled the tree branches and the tall grass of an open field, Von always believed that *yes,* it had really been *her* quim.

The side door of the Electra Complex sprang open. Angelique emerged at 9:35 for a smoke, par for the course when she was on backroom suck detail. She wore what counted as her costume—a white, easily removable shift. She kept a bare foot wedged in the door so it wouldn't shut; the door locked automatically.

"Showtime," Von announced. He and Greg stepped out of Greg's Nova. Through the crack in the door, they could faintly hear an old Celtic Frost song: "Return to the Eve."

Angelique had the bored detachment perfected by all veteran strippers, and she looked even less pleased to have visitors. It didn't detract too much from her beauty, though. Gentleman might prefer blonds, but there weren't many gentleman in a place like this, and her black hair was duly worshipped.

"We were hoping you could settle a bet between us," Von began.

The smile faltered on Greg's face. "We were?"

Von shot him an irritated look and prepared to continue his ploy. He surreptitiously craned his head around, searching for any stragglers in the parking lot. It was early in the evening, and the major activity wouldn't start for another couple hours. It wasn't a good idea to go to a strip show when the doors opened; by midnight you'd see your whole paycheck fluttering in some Jezebel's g-string.

Angelique waited, taking another drag on her cigarette.

"We wanted to know if you could smoke that cigarette with . . . well, what a learned man would call your 'netherlips.'"

Von glanced at his friend. "Ain't that right, Greg?"

Greg was practically drooling. "Right as rain, son!"

Angelique stared at them with a mixture of doubt and incredulity. "You want me to smoke with my box? For how much?"

"How much?" Von echoed. "Why, on the house, darling. In the interest of science."

"F.O.C.?" No doubt in her face now, just incredulity. "That's sick."

"Why, are you a dyke or something?"

Greg looked confused all over again. "What's . . . fawk?"

Angelique sighed. "You boys haven't even paid the cover, have you? Look, this is a business, not a charity. You want something extra, use the ATM inside. Then talk to me. Assuming you aren't cops."

Von's foot shot out and kicked the door, shattering the knob of bone above her heel. She crumpled, cigarette falling from her lips, crying out. It was doubtful anyone would hear her scream over Celtic Frost, but Von hurried, dragging her inside by her hair. Greg followed close behind, dropping a boot in her sternum. The vestiges of her last cigarette drag exploded as smoke from her mouth, followed instantly by a stream of vomit. The torrent was clogged with a murky, mucusy substance instantly recognizable as semen. Von pushed her head at the doorframe and slammed the door on it for good measure. She was definitely unconscious now. As far as the rest of the evening's activities were concerned she was not imperative, but this did not stop Von from stashing her in the Nova's trunk while Greg held the door. Old habits die hard.

Their destination in the Complex was fortuitously close, known as The Vacuum. It was actually two rooms, with holes in the dividing wall. The guys would not know who was behind the wall, but they'd slip forty bucks through for a blow job from whomever.

Greg gestured to an unassuming door, painted a sickly shade of green. "This is it."

Von nodded. "That's where the magic happens. Ready to meet the Wizard?"

Greg opened the door. They were tensed and ready to lay waste to anyone who might be within, but the room was empty. Angelique had been alone as calculated. There were bouncers at the club, but not as much of a call for them in a locked room. They guarded the door to get in here from inside the club, though, and it wouldn't be wise to lollygag . . . The Vacuum existed for an entirely different form of gagging.

"Man, did you see how much ball sauce she puked?" Greg marveled.

"Enough to repopulate the Holocaust," Von concurred. "I didn't think they really swallowed, even for the extra fiver. I don't about you, but I was relieved to find out there's actually a girl back here and not some candy-ass."

Von cracked his knuckles, pacing. He didn't want to be here a minute longer than he had to, but this part wasn't up to them, unfortunately.

They were not in a room so much as a storage closet. The distinguishing characteristic was of course the deadbolt-sized holes in the wall, in a descending arc—a convenience for the abnormally tall and short knob-job seekers. A sixty-watt bulb burned weakly overhead. A well-thumbed issue of *Shocking Crimes* had been left on a folding chair in front of the holes, presumably by Angelique. Von reached for it, catching a bold yellow headline which proclaimed ON THE TRAIL OF ATLANTA'S BUTT SEX KILLER! He'd heard about those goings-on, which imparted a profound moral to all aware of the murders—stay the hell out of Atlanta. A journalist named Thorndike McHatchet had the low-down on this sickening affair, as well as an amusing article entitled RAPIST CROSSED THE LINE TO MURDER, AND THEN WENT BACK TO RAPING AGAIN . . . WITH THE SAME VICTIM!

That's when he heard the door open on the other side of the wall. He looked up at Greg, startled, although he'd been expecting it. "Give me the knife," he whispered.

He glanced at the issue of *Shocking Crime* a little forlornly, and then stuffed the magazine into the front of his pants as a souvenir, his hands shaking.

The music within the club stopped long enough for them to both hear a fly unzip, and then two rolled up twenties were pushed through one of the holes. After a moment of indecision, the consumer slid another five dollars through. Greg pocketed the money.

Von held his hand out for the knife, waving his fingers. Greg put something in it; it was a Swiss army knife. Von's eyes flew open like window blinds. He got close to Greg's ear and whispered as loudly as he dared, "Are you out of your mind? We're not lost in the woods on a camping trip, you retard!"

"It's all I've got," Greg shot back.

The customer cleared his throat impatiently. Von looked down, and sure enough, the guy had eased his meat through one of the holes.

He gave Greg another disgusted look, and flicked out the Swiss army blade. He noted the faint beginnings of rust along its edge as he tentatively reached for the man's engorged member, like a timid schoolgirl picking up a dead frog for dissection in a biology lab. It jumped in his hand when he finally seized it, and the guy moaned.

Von's skin crawled, but the sleaze element was what had allowed for this whole caper in the first place after an amusing anecdote shared by a friend of theirs who got blown away just a few weeks ago, minding his own business at a stop light on the street corner of 37th and Garren as he walked home from the Electra Complex. The whole thing had been his idea, but he obviously didn't have any use for it now after a shotgun blast to the face courtesy of some whack job Greg claimed to know from Movie Heaven. The fact that he had only been kidding when he said it was no deterrent to Von and Greg, who practically had dollar signs in their eyes.

"Use your teeth," the man behind the wall gasped. "Please. I'll pay extra—"

The request came as no surprise, but it still made him feel queasy, like those magazines where fellas wanted a high heel crammed in their dickhole.

In a passable falsetto, Von asked him to lean into the wall. The customer obeyed. Von had the knife poised over the base of the shaft like a guillotine. The touch of blade on skin earned a groan that almost made Von physically ill. The tendons in his forearm tightened as he gripped tightly and began sawing with the army knife.

"Oh, baby . . . that's so sweet it's almost painf—" And then the guy dispensed with the "almost" diagnosis and began bleating like a slaughtered lamb. The rust made the cutting a grueling process, and Von had to keep the organ in an ironclad grip while his other hand burrowed through the shaft. He did an admirable job of working from the initial wound, like a lumberjack burying his axe in the same groove swing after swing. The blood was deep red, gushing from the stump-in-progress like a surrogate orgasm. The guy struggled as his screams became almost feminine shrieks, which however heart-felt and desperate could not exceed the volume of "Too Fast for Love" on the club speakers. His knees had given out, but the member in Von's hand could only elongate as the customer pushed off from the wall, trying to squirm free. Once the rusted blade had slit and hacked through enough of the shaft, the frantic gyration provided the final ingredient to the castration. The last inch and a quarter came free in a moist surge of ripping meat and veins.

Von stumbled backward, dropping genitalia and implement alike. A renewed spray of crimson jetted through the suck-hole and then through two more of the descending holes as the newly minted eunuch pitched over to his right and hit the deck, a faint thud barely audible on the other side of the wall and undoubtedly lost to the nearest bouncer beyond the door.

"Come on!' Greg seized the severed sex organ and bolted.

Von slipped in the haphazard puddles of blood, but his sudden paranoia that Greg was trying to make off with the penis gave him the proper coordination to stand erect. He grabbed the knife with a blood-soaked hand and tore off after Greg. He was quick enough to catch the side door before it slammed shut behind his companion, and he emerged into a stifling wall of humidity.

Greg was tearing through his pockets in a mad search for his keys. The contraband was slumped on the roof, losing rigidity as blood tapered out and slid down the driver's side window.

"I can't find them!" he shouted in panic.

Von felt something uncomfortable digging at his thigh, and remembered he'd last used the keys to open the trunk for Angelique. He dug them out and tossed them over the roof to Greg, who dropped them in his haste. Four attempts later, the key slid in. Greg bounced across the seat to unlock Von's side. Von was shutting his door as Greg turned the ignition, and Greg didn't even pause to slam his own door until he was peeling out.

"Slow down!" Von snapped. "People act crazy trying to get *in* to a titty bar, not out!"

Greg eased up all of five miles per hour, gunning for the exit. He came dangerously close to sideswiping a Civic before hooking a right. The horn of the other car faded, though the driver raised a middle finger for good measure. Greg remained oblivious to the whole sequence, painfully unaware how close he'd come to blowing the whole deal. "We did it!" he whooped. "The most daring tool theft ever!"

"We'll need to clean that blood off the windows soon as we get to some back roads," Von said, praying the Civic didn't chase after them. He glanced backward until he was sure there would be no road rage retaliation, his head almost lighter than air. The millwork of his veins and arteries decided to do their thing again. He exhaled and resumed his train of thought. "We'd never be able to explain to some pig why holy mother of God, *what did you do with it, Greg?*" He jumped around in his seat as though stung on the ass, looking behind him, beneath him, below him. "It's not here! We lost it!"

Greg plowed the brake pedal with both feet, the tires screeching and the body swerving uncertainly. He pulled an illegal U-turn into the thankfully empty oncoming road and punched the accelerator, hanging a left back onto Seymour Street and past a Burger King. The Electra Complex grew bigger, like a mouth about to swallow them.

"It's by the back door!" Greg reasoned. "We didn't bring it in after I set it on the roof, and it must've fell off."

"*We* didn't bring it in?" Von echoed. "You mean *you* didn't bring it in!"

Greg had no reply for that as he barreled through the parking lot to approximately where they had had been before. "Shit, hang on," he said as Von reached for the door handle. "There's no light back here." He put it back in reverse and flipped on the high beams. The car hitched slightly before it came to a stop.

Greg sprang out of the Nova, searching the lot frantically. Von moved more slowly, as though weighed down by a heavy heart. He immediately walked in front of the car, into the glare of the headlights, and quietly said, "Here."

Greg followed Von's gaze and gasped in horror.

"That's our jillion dollars," Von said, pointing. "You just made road kill out of our meal ticket, sumbitch."

Greg dropped to his knees in horror and disbelief. His dramatic collapse afforded him a closer look, which he held as though the organ would regenerate back to its original— and surely pricier—form. The member was curiously white now, all its blood shot through the vessels and glans by the weight of the car; white except for the distinctive treads of Michelin tires. What had been inserted through the suck-hole just minutes ago now resembled something you'd fling on a plate with a spatula and douse with maple syrup.

"We gotta get outta here," Von announced. "We can't let him know we got nothing to bargain with. We'll have to take it with us."

"Him" was Edward Rochester, the latest addition to the men's soprano choir. He blew a thousand bucks a night at the Complex, and seemed to arrive in a different luxury car each time. On Saturdays at 9:45, he always visited the Vacuum. Even a destitute man would find five million dollars an agreeable price for his lovewand, so Von and Greg figured Edward would be only too happy to ante up—and right quick at that. Every second counted.

Greg gave Von a doubtful look, but made talons of his fingers and tried to slip them between the flattened organ and the asphalt. Von worked the other side. It was like trying to peel the label off a packaging envelope—getting a sizable piece to come up with no problem and then losing it as it tore from its body. The member was the same way, a smidgen of flesh peeling off like masking tape, then dissolving into a cluster of various strands like bubble-gum stuck to the bottom of a shoe.

They kept an eye out for approaching cars or patrons making an early exit, but their luck held (the setback of the squashed sexual apparatus notwithstanding).

Von forced the silly putty-like chunks into his pockets, thinking this was one time he'd be sure to use the laundromat.

Edward Rochester was in a great deal of pain. He'd pay to have the bastard tortured. The seediness of the Complex appealed to him in ways the higher class "gentlemen's' clubs" could not, but he could have done without getting his ass kicked by an uncultured patron. He'd made the apparently ghastly error of knocking somebody's bottle of beer off their table when trying to negotiate his way from near the stage to the door to the Vacuum. Before he even had a chance to offer to pay for a new one, the bearded patron said, "Watch where the fuck you're going, dicksucker!" and pushed him into the wall. Edward rebounded from it, air whooshing from his lungs, and stepped into a right hook. A few kicks found him as he tasted the floor, and he began to worry that the strobe light effect he was seeing wasn't part of the stage show this time. It actually was, fortunately, but he and Russell Crowe were separated by interchangeable bald men in black shirts emblazoned with white letters reading SECURITY and dragged out of the club. Hence, he'd missed his 9:45 "appointment" with Angelique . . .

In greater pain was Horace Cromwell, who'd given plasma just to treat himself to a good beejay. And now he was convulsing on the filthy floor of the Vacuum, forty-five dollars and one penis poorer.

No one could hear his screams over the music; not that he wanted anyone to find out what had become of his girth. What he did want was revenge. He'd have it before the night was over . . . if he didn't bleed to death.

The Bic lighter cost him all of a dollar, but it was reliable. It flamed on, first try. He didn't want to look at the stump, at the mangled roots of what had given him so much pleasure and disappointed so many girls since high school. It was like looking at a tangle of circuitry spooling from an open wall socket. He could feel his pulse in the mess of severed blood vessels, a renewal of pain with each pounding beat. Blood matted his thighs like he'd just given birth, and he probably didn't have much more he could waste.

He was telling his hand *No!* even as it brought the lighter closer. The searing heat was close enough to scald the blood and torn skin, discomforting and nearly agonizing. Horace gritted his teeth and brought the flame home.

If he'd been in pain before, he was in Hell now. An electric current of agony erupted in his groin, his original pain with a whole battalion of reinforcements. He felt every orifice knot up as if to contain the sparks shooting through his nerves. The world became a vision of fire and only a chaotic scream with no beginning or end as the soundtrack. He pierced the veil only in brief flashes of reality, as if he could only bear glimpses without losing his mind. When he

91

could finally align his vision with the grim reality, he saw the ultimate parody of male human reproduction—a blackened, smoking gorge of a stump. He fancied that he still heard the sizzling of the veins as they cauterized and stemmed the flow of blood, a morbid sound and odor he knew he could expect to be waiting for him in dreams, waking him up in the dead of night.

He vomited convulsively into his lap, whether from the tidal wave of pain or the reek of his own smoldered crotch he could not say. Some of the bile caught in his stub, and mildly bubbled from the heat. He thought he might have passed out at some point, but wasn't sure.

He crawled to the door and unlocked it. Someone was waiting outside.

An animated customer greeted him, eyes wide with admiration. "Dude! That must have been the best nut ever, you screamed like a yodeler caught in a thresh machine!"

Horace staggered past, trying to button his pants. He could still hear his genitals crackling. The new arrival gave an astonished gasp behind him at the sight of all the blood in the Vacuum.

Horace followed the trail of his blood to a back exit, just in time to see them leave in the Nova. Hunched over and groaning miserably, he ambled toward his car.

"What's he gonna do, ask to talk to it?" Von asked, maybe trying to convince himself more than Greg. "Make sure it's still alive? He'll leap at any chance to get it. We'll take his money and shoot him in the back. It won't be the worst thing that ever happened to him, now, will it?"

"Good plan, king," Greg complimented.

"I just hope Sammy doesn't act crazy tonight. That boy ain't all there."

Greg nodded uneasily, even as he drove them to Sammy's house. Neither of them ever knew what to expect from Sammy, and they'd already had one bad surprise this evening as it was. It seemed a bad omen of the shape of things to come . . . and the night hadn't even really begun.

92

Part II: Slut Necro Lambda and The Divided Man

Sammy feverishly worked his inches, member in one hand and his mother's soiled undergarments in the other. He ejaculated into a tube sock with faded yellow stripes and an increasingly cardboard-like texture. He supposed he could have used Mom's underwear, but that was just sort of sick, the way he figured. It was a show of respect. He shuddered in the aftermath, smothering his nose and mouth with the panties, inhaling the musky dampness. It was almost enough to stiffen him again—three more today would make a baker's dozen—but he would have company soon. There were other tasks to perform.

He gingerly removed the tube sock. As he feared, the friction had caused his sores to run. It was probably to be expected after so many transmissions today; you pay to play. Off-white streams of pus ran in rivulets down his shaft, erupting from the tiny mouth-like lesions. The accompanying agony (including a gasp-inducing, white fire painful sensation while urinating) and random discharges concerned him. At times, it was downright unbearable.

Probably something he ate, he figured. Lotta bacteria out there. It would pass. It sure was taking its sweet time, though. He didn't want to contemplate the day when it would be more trouble than it was worth to jack down. A man should have a fake tooth hollowed out with a cyanide tablet in such an event—break in case of emergency.

Behind him, the Divided Man stood sentinel. From the attic, a thumping sound. And from below, feeble screams from the basement.

Sammy chuckled as he pulled up his pants, wincing a bit the complaint of his sores. He addressed the Divided Man. "If they thought before was bad, they're gonna *love* what happens next."

The paring knife appeared slight, but for all the caterwauling it provoked as it carved out Mary Jane Turner's anus, it may as well have been a jackhammer. The girl was too weak to lift her head a scant five minutes ago, but now she was flailing from the meat hook like a speared fish. The other sluts were about as vocal as they witnessed the excision—still capable of being shocked after months of imprisonment and experiments that made Josef Mengele look like Dr. Spock.

Surgery to Sammy was art, and the more involuntary the better. He was damned good at it. On the rare occasions that perverted fantasies of his mother (often they were technically *memories*) failed to shove a beat-off session past the finish line, he'd remember the screams of Linda Gordon (missing 01/27/2000) as she awoke to find a Labrador retriever's head (missing 07/17/2000) sewn to her shoulder, its tongue dangling to her nipple. On the heels of that, she discovered the dog's tail had been power-stapled between her buttocks. Sammy had been unable to do anything with poor Spot's doghood, so he placed it on a saucer and told Linda, "Bon appétit!" She was understandably reluctant, but her hunger weakened her resolve three days later. By then, the bubblegum-pink "cocktail," as he liked to think of it, was collecting a rather devoted congregation of flies. She scarfed it down like a real trouper . . . and was then served another, this from a poodle (missing 07/23/2000). She failed to learn her lesson and waited again, vowing she would not succumb this time, would not afford him any more of her dignity. Whitney Houston would have been proud. She lasted four days, and then pitifully brushed away the flies and dropped it in her mouth like a popcorn shrimp. Linda wasn't so successful at chowing down for Old Glory this time, though, and her quease gland was wrung like a chicken neck. Shriveled giblets of flyblown dog dick and chyme were rerouted up her gullet in a powerful deluge that doubled her over with sobs, regurgitant flecks stuck in the fur of the Labrador's head (Sammy didn't care very much for poodles either, admittedly).

Yes, thinking about her ordeal could fill a tube sock faster than you could recite your social security number.

Linda was a remarkable accomplishment and would have been a primo addition to anyone's resume, but the piece de resistance was undoubtedly Sheryl Gray, with contribution from her fellow sorority sisters. Slut Necro Lambda, he called it. The endeavor had been a real challenge. The removal of five vaginas took two days, a painstaking process of careful cutting and hacking. He'd botched a sixth attempt, which would have been a complete waste had Von and Greg not volunteered to take her off his hands. A prone Sheryl was then the recipient of the world's first multi-vaginal transplant. Rather crude exploratory surgery techniques freed enough room for the canals, in effect becoming makeshift passages to her digestive system in most instances. Removal of bone segments allowed for more slightly varied installations of these surrogate fuckholes. Sheryl did not survive this radical procedure, regrettably . . . but that was merely the final ingredient to the thrill.

This unparalleled success earned him the esteemed title of Doctor Butcher from Von and Greg. Sammy let them have a turn with Slut Necro Lambda, under the stipulation that they both had to use the same orifice. Why not? He had plenty to spare. And he still had plenty afterward—the crazy bastards had used the backdoor. It defeated the whole purpose of the operation, but that was Von and Greg for you.

Back to the business at hand, Sammy couldn't help but notice Mary Jane Turner's anus looked like the underside of a mushroom. He was puzzling over whether or not this was erotic, and why the incising sounded like nothing more exotic than the dicing of a tomato. This was for culinary purposes, of course, but you'd expect a more significant soundtrack to accompany the theft of someone's asshole. The flesh could be so banal, even with artistry like Sammy's to spice it up.

The incision came full circle and the perimeter dropped out. Sammy peeled it off the floor, though not before fully appreciating the anatomical delights he'd uncovered. A more educated person could probably shoot out five syllable terminologies for everything, but to Sammy, it was just glistening and rather stringy rectal meat dripping like a melting icicle.

It reminded him of a pornographic movie called *Gaping Anus,* naturally enough. The exposed muscle tissue would be slick and very inviting, like a mitten stuffed with Vaseline. Maybe he could even perform without bursting any more sores. This was all extremely enticing, but it wasn't like she was going anywhere anyway. Besides, he had the attic to think of now.

He left the cellar and his little mascots—a stripper, a prostitute, two college girls (with only one anus between them now) and a nurse—all worthless whores, in other words—and climbed the stairs back up to the kitchen. He set the souvenir from Mary Jane on the chopping block, employing his thumb to slide it from fingers—it stuck like mucus. He plucked up his mallet and brought it down, effectively squashing the wrinkled flesh. From a Tupperware bowl, he produced the remaining cuts of Sue Harper's buttocks (additional remains recovered 05/11/2002, 05/25/2002 and 06/02/2002), and cranked them through an old fashioned meat-grinder onto a paper plate. A spatula freed the compacted meat from the chopping block, which Sammy scraped on the paper plate. He threw it into the microwave and set it on high, whistling all the while.

The thumping in the attic grew more persistent in anticipation of feeding time. He heard Greg's Nova in the driveway as the microwave beeped its conclusion. He rushed upstairs to make the delivery. He hadn't bothered to wash his hands since handling Mom's underwear (and himself), he realized. Sammy laughed at his carelessness. He unlocked the attic door, chucked the meat inside, and relocked the door from the outside. He heard scraping sounds as the occupant crawled to the newly arrived meal. It would taste like arse, but that was pretty much the point.

Sammy was scrambling back downstairs when Von and Greg walked in. Both parties had their own reasons to distract the other. Sammy came up with the first diversion. "You're late," he accused, short of breath.

Von was grateful for the opportunity to stall. "Why you breathing so hard? You just get done jackin' down?"

"I was upstairs."

"Upstairs jackin' down?" Von pounced.

Sammy ignored him. "What's the matter with you two? You look like Gillian Anderson died and had her remains cremated before you got a crack at her in the morgue."

Von sighed heavily, feigning a sudden interest in the orange carpet of the den. It was an ugly concoction that looked to have been stitched together from skinned Muppets.

"You two morons didn't get it, did you? The guy practically gave you his dick on a silver platter and you didn't take it. Unbelievable."

"That ain't what happened, fag face," Von shouted back. "We did the whole thing the way we talked about, no problem. It was easier than snatching a Latch-Key Kid."

Sammy didn't speak for a moment, puzzled. "Okay . . . *was* Gillian Anderson cremated?"

"Nuh-uh." Von sighed again. "Look, we got in, got the package, and got the hell out. It was going great." Von gave his cohort a disgusted look. "Until Mario Andretti over here peeled out on the prize."

"I said I was sorry!" Greg protested, even though he'd done no such thing.

"Sorry doesn't take the pieces of Rochester's dick out of our pockets and make it whole again!"

Sammy didn't bother to hold in his laughter. "You got a rocket in your pocket, Von?"

"Come on, this ain't something to joke about. Rochester finds out Greg ruined it, he'll use that ransom money to have us killed."

"So don't tell him. He's not going to report you to the Better Business Bureau."

"But what if he insists on seeing it first?"

"Knowing every second counts, that would take balls."

"He's still got those," Greg pointed out.

"What about you, Sammy?" Von asked hopefully. "You got an extra one stashed around here someplace?"

"Oh yeah, sure, just check the candy bowl on the refrigerator. Of course I don't. I don't kill guys. What do you think I am, a gay?"

"No, but—" Von paused. "Wait a minute now. Me and

Greg's killed us a few dudes before. You trying to say that makes us rope smokers?"

"Not necessarily—"

"Because Greg's the one who did all the killing, so he's the damn queer."

"Hey, you're the one who had you a handful of Rochester's pork sword," Greg pointed out.

"Shut the hell up, Greg."

"Yeah, Sammy, he was asking Von to use his teeth and everything!"

"Shut the hell up, Greg!"

"Both of you calm down," Sammy interjected. "And it's actually good that you remember these details. You'll be able to prove beyond a doubt that you're the ones who did it."

"Oh right, I'm sure there'll be all sorts of cranks lining up to take the credit for it."

"Would you just hand someone three million dollars because they claimed to have your most prized possession? If it was me, I'm not sure I'd take the word of a dick thief at face value . . . especially one who's a closet homo."

"Hey, I thought we were getting—" Greg began.

Von cut him off with remarkable subtlety. "Shut the hell up, *Greg*!"

Sammy might have noticed, but a succession of thumping noises overhead mercifully distracted him and grabbed his attention. "I'll be right back," he offered and stormed up the staircase.

When he was out of earshot, Von grabbed a handful of Greg's shirt. "Do you need a written invitation before you'll use your brain?"

"What?"

"What were you just about to say? That you thought we were getting *five* million dollars, not three?"

"Well, aren't we?"

"Yeah. And how much money do you think Sammy'll want if he finds out?"

"He don't deserve any of it . . . you and me are the ones doing all the work!"

"Exactly. But a man with Rochester's money can pay to create a lot of problems for us. Like . . . hell, I don't know, ninjas and shit."

Greg gave this possibility a moment of reverent silence.

"So we might need his help after all. And we need his house to arrange the ransom. We don't want to be seen anywhere near our homes, just in case."

"But what could Sammy do against ninjas?"

Von considered this and shrugged. "This is Doctor Butcher we're talking about, Greg. Those invisible bastards could be pissing throwing stars for the rest of their lives, which probably wouldn't be very long if they try to get between us and that money."

Greg looked up the stairwell, listening for Sammy. When he didn't hear any sign that he was returning, he said, "I've got a better idea."

Von was skeptical, to say the least.

"What if we kill Sammy?" Greg whispered, so quietly Von almost didn't hear him.

"Say . . . that ain't half-bad," Von considered. "We get Sammy, we can cut him off and have a replacement dick. Rochester won't be able to tell the difference."

"Hey, that didn't even occur to me," Greg admitted.

"Then we can have his house at no charge, and we don't have to share any of the money with him."

"I didn't think of that either! That's even better!"

"Then why the hell did you suggest it in the first place? You must like killing other guys and dominating 'em. Sammy's right, you probably are gay."

"The hell you say! I was thinking with Sammy out of the picture, we'd have Slut Necro Lambda and all those whores downstairs all to ourselves! That's just as good as five million dollars, you ask me!"

"Slut Necro Lambda," Von repeated with earnest reverence. "Man, I could certainly use some more of that backdoor action, no doubt about it."

Greg grinned. "Now who sounds like the damn queer?"

At that moment, they heard more noises overhead and

99

what had to be Sammy's voice, the words inaudible but apparently forceful.

"Did he move all those twats up to the attic?" Von asked.

"I doubt it. I think I can hear 'em crying in the basement."

"Hmm. Maybe we should go find out, don't you think? He shouldn't be keeping any secrets from us. We're supposed to be partners."

Greg nodded. "You got that right, son. We can't abide by no traitor. I'll tell him that when we slash his throat for him."

Von gestured to follow and began to quietly ascend the stairs.

Horace followed the Nova to a secluded two story home on an unmarked and unpaved road off Connelly Trail. The woods were thicker here, and it looked like the kind of place where toothless bumpkins would command you to squeal like a pig before bending you over and breaking you off. At this point, he was quite confident that the worst that could possibly happen to him *had* happened to him, and any subsequent cuts, bruises, and ass-poundings would be trivial at best.

When you had to crack the window of your Rabbit because the mephitic fetor of your crispified cock stump was nauseating you virtually to the point of unconsciousness, you didn't have much further to fall. It triggered a very old memory from his childhood, an evening when his mother had melted a plastic ladle in the dishwasher, creating an overpowering olfactory assault so abominable that he'd had to seek refuse in the basement to keep from puking.

He stopped a hundred yards from the house, his headlights extinguished. He'd go the rest of the way on foot and hopefully get the drop on them. He had to wait for his eyes to adjust, although it still didn't afford much definition to his environment. Out here was the kind of true darkness of night unknown to the city, away from all the street lights and neon, with even the stars blotted out by the heavy canopy of the trees overhead. The orange glow from the windows ahead was his only guiding light.

Was this even their house? Was his manhood being utilized in some form of ritual satanic abuse? Were they perhaps religious fanatics exacting the vengeance of their god on the "impure" heathens who sought the earthly pleasures of the flesh?

If so, it might be time their little sect learned the doctrine of an eye for an eye . . . and a life for a cock.

They found the Divided Man midway through the ascent. Greg saw him first and stopped cold. His hand seemed to have a mind of its own as it reached out and tugged at Von's sleeve, never turning his head from the sight. Von was more eager to get upstairs and find out exactly what was so secretive that Sammy couldn't tell them about it, and almost pulled a "Jump back, boy, you're botherin' me," on him. Greg, however, was insistent, and Von finally peered back around the corner of the room they'd just passed on the way to the attic stairs.

"The hell?" Von asked. In that moment he wouldn't haven't been able to say why they had been so determined to get to the attic, or what the hell an attic was in the first place. Greg was still stretching his sleeve to get him to look, but he didn't notice (neither, for that matter, did Greg).

It was the parents' bedroom. Von always assumed Sammy's mom and dad were both dead, especially considering the extent of their son's homicidal forays into surgical possibilities. The evidence on display didn't disprove his theory, but initially it appeared like a locked room aficionado's wet dream. Cast randomly on the carpet were a lady's undergarments (pock-marked with dried droplets of menstrual blood) and a tube sock with no equal. Beyond those, statuesque against the far wall was the upright body of a man. A network of wires had been run through an eyelet from the ceiling to keep the body in a standing position. The wire work had turned him into a puppet of flesh, bone, and organs. His torso had been cleanly divided from throat to stomach, the corner flaps of the skin held aside by surgical clamps. This strategic sculpting allowed for a view of the man's entrails, which remained stationary against the demand of gravity due to its slightly slumped position, unmolested by any incisions or perforations. Their arrangement seemed as aesthetically-conscious as the objects in a still-life drawing, a measured integration of reds and yellows.

His sex organs had not been surgically inspected.

"You know what this means," Von whispered.

Greg nodded. "Sure do! Sammy's a homo, son!"

Von barely refrained from slapping him. "It *means* we have a placement for Rochester. We won't have to cut Sammy out after all."

Greg considered this a moment, then nodded again. His attention fell on the sock and he stooped to pick it up, apparently already distracted from the wonder of the Divided Man. "You ready for Sock Puppet Theater?" he asked mischievously. Before Von could tell him to put a sock in it, Greg forced his hand into the sock, already bending his wrist to form an elongated mouth with his hand.

He frowned instantly. "Yuck . . . it's all wet inside."

"Three guesses why, and the first two don't count, slick." Von gestured to the soiled panties discarded on the floor.

Greg looked at him blankly.

"Why the hell else do you think a man would leave a sock lying around on the bedroom floor, you ijit?" Von asked rhetorically. Then, because he understood the futility of asking Greg to make a mental leap of any kind, he answered anyway. "Sammy was filling it up with his rocket sauce, son!"

"*Shit!*" Greg palmed his forearm and yanked the sock away like someone trying to haul a tablecloth away without upsetting everything on top of it. The sock dropped to the carpet inside out, and Greg jumped back from it like it was a rattlesnake. He wadded up a bedspread and dried his arm off, never taking his eye away from the sock, as though terrified that it would jump up and try to pull itself back up his arm.

Von chuckled, but as quietly as he could, still listening for the sound of Sammy's returning footsteps. They hadn't heard anything from the attic for a few moments. He dug the Swiss army knife from his pocket and recoiled at the feel of the moist clumps of Rochester's original tool. "I got the last one, boss man. This is all you."

Greg accepted the knife a bit uncertainly.

"Get crackin', man," Von said. "He'll be back any minute now. I'll keep a look-out."

Greg extracted the knife blade and walked over to the strung-up cadaver. This close up, he noticed the eyes were open. The lids had been removed. That was a trademark Sammy maneuver, just in case Greg had any shred of hope left that Sammy had nothing to do with this *objet d'art* displayed in the bedroom. He and Von had been up here before, but the door had always been closed. They'd never paid it any mind. Greg started trying to remember if there were any *other* doors that had always been closed to them in the past.

Just the attic.

He knelt before the Divided Man, thinking it was pretty sick of Sammy to have some naked dude with his guts on display. That girl with the dog head and tail, that would have been far more appropriate.

"Hurry!" Von commanded from the doorway. "He could come down any second now!"

Greg winced as though the tube sock misadventure was happening all over again. He reached for the man's groin and grasped. The effect was instantaneous—the slop of immobile entrails squirmed free, a minor avalanche of the digestive tract right over Greg's hands and into his lap. He sprang back, dropping the coils which had slickly gathered over his thighs onto the shag carpet with a surprisingly heavy slapping sound.

Their eyes both shot up to the ceiling as though it would dematerialize to reveal Sammy. When it did not, Von jabbed a finger in Greg's direction. "Get your ass back over there and find it!"

Greg gave him a helpless look, like a little kid whose trail of bread crumbs had been eaten up by the ravens.

"Now!" Von snapped, somehow managing a scream at whisper level. He wasn't sure Sammy would go ballistic over this, but since Sammy kept the Divided Man a secret, there might be some sentimental value attached to him. He'd undoubtedly notice the "alterations," but maybe not before they were a few million dollars richer. And if he blew the whole episode out of proportion, they still had the option of killing him. They just better make sure that they got it right, because they would probably only get one shot at it. And obviously the guy wasn't above surgical liberties with the male figure after all.

Greg had to step into the pile of entrails to get close enough. They squelched under his shoes. His left foot nearly slid out from under him as he tested the terrain like someone on a frozen pond. A length of intestine burst under his inquisitive weight. He reached into the obscuring mess still attached to the abdominal cavity. Everything felt like wet snakes. He had to extend his fingers and specifically pull aside various coils like vertical blinds, trying to uncover the crotch again. Finally irritated, he grabbed a fistful and yanked them like the starting cord to a lawnmower. They tore and spattered him with digestive juice. He tossed them over his shoulder and grabbed another handful. One of the cords holding the cadaver upright snapped. The Divided Man started to tilt, unbalanced, so Greg held him up with one hand as he withdrew more yellowish ropes from the other. He found what he was looking for, and then had to lean up against the body to keep it situated as he carved. It went easily, having expired soft. Greg closed his hand on it and stepped out of the gut pile. The body collapsed, its arms draping over Greg as though hugging him.

"Mission accomplished," Greg reported, pushing the cadaver away from him. It struck the ground, face up.

Von shook his head. "You know what you look like?"

Greg gave himself a quick once-over. "No, what?"

"You look like a guy who just stepped in a heap of guts, tore some more out for good measure, and then sliced off a dead man's wang with a Swiss army knife."

104

"So you think Sammy'll notice?"

"Only if he doesn't fall down the stairs, break his neck, and die before he sees you again."

As if on cue, the attic door slammed shut overhead and footsteps announced Sammy's inexorable return. He did not fall down the stairs, break his neck, and die. He walked past the room, stopped, backtracked, did a visible double-take, and began to take inventory of the extensive damage.

The first thing he said was, "Why is that tube sock inside out?"

"Uh . . . it was like that when we got here," Greg offered, the picture of innocence if that picture had a cracked frame. And no picture.

"Yeah," Von agreed, painfully aware that they didn't actually formulate any plans on how to take Sammy out. They had acted under the assumption that they would acquire the genitalia and then simply become the vessels for divine inspiration. They had a Swiss army knife between them and no powers of telepathy to coordinate exactly what to do with it.

Sammy had moved on from the tube sock to the mess of gore beyond it.

"The body was already like that, too," Von said. "When we got here, I mean."

"Uh huh," Sammy said without tone. "Funny how that worked out, seeing as how it was perfectly fine when I walked past a few minutes ago . . . the body perfectly upright, the entrails neatly in place . . . the tube sock correctly oriented."

Von remained silent, waiting for his associate to volunteer a predictably pathetic excuse. Greg did the same. An awkward silence stretched its legs.

"What's that you got in your hand, Greg?" Sammy finally asked.

Greg hadn't looked this surprised since his sister caught him masturbating in the shower (but slightly less so than when she'd hopped in and taken over the shucking responsibilities for him). He struggled for a good answer. What he found was, "Just . . . just some . . . gum. Like you . . . chew?"

Sammy smiled. "So chew then, Greg old buddy. Don't let me stop you."

"Yeah, Greg," Von agreed. "Chew."

If he'd been lost in the forest before, he was going into the oven now.

"Greg, you have the rare distinction of running over one man's junk and disemboweling a cadaver while trying to procure a changeling penis, all within about 30 minutes," Sammy said. "And you ruined a work of art in the process. So if you don't start chewing in the next ten seconds, I'm going to tear you a brand new asshole, 'son.' And I will use all my surgical know-how to make sure that you live long enough to use it, too."

Greg chewed. It may not have even been the most unpleasant experience in his life from the layman's perspective (lest we forget other extracurricular activities with corpses, though female, whose every orifice he had lunched on, and ravenously at that), but it was altogether more humbling.

"Oh, hell," he said between mouthfuls. "It's . . . it's really chewy, guys . . . Christ on a unicycle, it's so damn *chewy ...*"

It was not hyperbole. His jaws worked mechanically, piston-like, to conclude this humiliation fast enough to break the sound barrier, but the morsels resisted. They bred in his mouth, tough as gristle with the texture of the fat on a steak. He could almost visualize each part as he chomped . . . the shaft, the head, the urethra, the veins, the erectile tissue. His own size seemed to wilt between his legs with each bite.

He cried as he ate.

"Fantastic," Sammy complimented. "You took it like man, Greg. I didn't think you had it in you . . . although I guess you do now, don't you? So now that I trust you two dopes have been exorcised of your little substitution fantasy, you can get your asses on the horn and start making demands to Mrs. Rochester. Unless vibrator companies have jumped into the telemarketing biz, you'll be the most welcome call of the night."

Greg's Adam's apple bobbed as he swallowed. He gagged miserably, but held it down.

"Hurry up and swig some Listerine, dickbreath," Sammy said. "The time is later than you think."

Part III: Embryonic Necropsy and Devourment

"Make sure you dumbasses hit star-six-seven when you call," Sammy admonished.

Von stood at the kitchen counter with the portable phone in his hand, reading over the "script" in front of him. Greg had prepared it, which in retrospect probably wasn't the best idea. Somehow it had seemed more important for Von to watch the latest installment of a porn series called *Gaping Anus* the other night rather than iron out the script with him. It was the 24th volume, but he had to hand it to them—they were finding ways to keep it fresh. You never knew which gal would start out with a nickel-sized rectal circumference that wound up more like the ball from a shot put three hours and forty-seven minutes later. It seemed like 4 hours well spent. All Greg had to do was incorporate the points he had outlined. He now understood that the word *Greg* should have stood out to him more in that scenario.

"Haven't you ever heard of punctuation?" Von finally asked, disgusted.

"Let me see that," Sammy said and snatched it away. "I don't know why you wasted your time coming up with this thing. You're trying to ransom her husband's junk, not sell her a magazine subscription." His brow crinkled as he read it for a few seconds, frown deepening. "He's right, Greg. It's not exactly Hemingway. This ain't even *Flowers for Algernon*. If you tried to read this to Mrs. Rochester word for word, she'd tell the police they oughtta narrow their search to guys with Down's syndrome."

"Or a retard," Von said.

Greg made no reply. He stood by the refrigerator, wincing at the sour taste in his mouth. Vomiting would be worse than the actual eating, though; all those masticated chunks of penile debris resurrected. The thought was horrifying, and the prospect felt more and more likely with each slosh of his disturbed stomach juices. He had to eliminate the taste.

"I've got to eat something else," he announced.

"Still hungry?" Sammy chuckled. "We could have Von turn out his pockets."

Greg opened the refrigerator, staring at the shelves like a man beholding an oasis in the desert. He reached in with both hands and removed a large Tupperware bowl, then started yanking open drawers, looking for a spoon or fork.

"Just help yourself," Sammy said, irritated.

Von took the script from Sammy and crumpled it up. "Hell with it. I'll make something up."

"Couldn't be any worse. Follow the subject with the predicate and it'll already be a vast improvement."

Greg peeled back the Tupperware lid and sank his spoon into a nearly gelatinous concoction of crimson slop and glistening lumps. He filled his mouth with it, grinning idiotically. "Fine eatin' here, Sammy. What is this, some kind of cobbler?"

"I believe the medical term is 'spontaneous abortion,'" Sammy replied.

Greg's grin froze on his face. He looked down at the bowl again, first seeing his rather awe-struck reflection caught by the light above him, and then the true texture of those lumps he'd first taken to be cobbler crust. The truth seemed obvious now. He prodded it with his spoon and discovered a runny film at the surface of the glop, like pond scum.

The amniotic sac . . . or what passed for it in its premature expulsion.

"There may be a few morsels of the placenta left," Sammy said, matter-of-factly. He could have been talking about the reds in a bowl of M&M's.

Von had paused with the phone in his hand the instant Sammy said "spontaneous abortion." He finally dared to speak. "You mean some whore had a miscarriage and squeezed all that slop out of her joytrail? And you tossed it in a bowl and froze it?"

Sammy nodded. "That's about the size of it."

Von processed this for a few seconds. "Well, hellfire,

Greg, why're you just standing there staring like that freak in *Sleepaway Camp?* Get me a spoon, too!"

Greg, hand held over his mouth, surrendered the bowl and spoon to Von without a word. He looked rather green around the gills.

"You're kidding, right?" Von asked, staring at the bowl. "I ain't using this spoon after you. You just had a dick in your mouth, son! I don't want no part of that."

"I rinsed my mouth out," Greg protested slowly, as though afraid more than words would escape through his lips if he spoke too fast.

Sammy intervened. "Are you two gonna debate dental hygiene all night, or are you gonna get this Rochester bitch on the horn?"

"Right now I'm a bit more interested in how you got ahold of this here tasty little *de*ssert," Von said. He dipped a thumb into the mess on the outer edge—where Greg's spoon probably hadn't explored—and slid it in his mouth. He sucked at it thoughtfully, one eyebrow arched, then moaned approvingly. Some of it remained smeared around his lips like clown make-up.

"How I wound up with a puddle of abortion in my refrigerator? It's kind of a boring story, really." Sammy shrugged, but agreed to enlighten. He could have been talking about vacation slides from a trip he hadn't really enjoyed. "I zapped this primo slut with my stun gun when she left the library, then brought her here. Slapped some meat down on her in so many different ways, I could have made my own cookbook. After a few weeks, her belly started expanding. I figured she was just bloated, but after awhile I realized there was a little Sammy on the way."

Von frowned. "How do you know she wasn't already pregnant?"

Sammy paused. "You know, I didn't even really consider that. She may have been carrying some stranger's child, at that. Well, I sure am glad that worthless skank is dead now. Got what she deserved."

"She's dead?"

"They don't make 'em much deader. I was pounding away at her ass like a jackhammer, and then I hear this tearing sound, right? So I pull back and look down, and there's this . . . Remember how the Play-Doh Factory had that thing where you cranked and all the stuff came out in four or five different clumps? It was like that, it just started oozing out of her and dropping on my lap. Kind of lukewarm. And I was thinking this was all a bit tragic cuz it was my kid—or at least I thought so at the time—so I tried to do the gentlemanly thing and hurry up and finish my nut, right? But she wasn't making it easy on me. All that thrashing around and resisting—hell, it's probably what cost her the little bastard in the first place. It was messed up, though, 'cause it was like every time I sent the battering ram home, more of that shit would squeeze out. To make a long story short, I went off, she went out, and the rest went in a Tupperware bowl to be served to—" He paused here, as though stopping himself from saying more than he intended. "For a special occasion."

Von caught the subterfuge. "Let's talk more about the noises in the attic."

"Yeah!" Greg echoed. "You got cops up there, waiting for us to make our ransom demand?"

"Yes, Greg, that's precisely it. With a basement practically wallpapered in women I've raped, tortured, and killed over the past seven years, the police couldn't wait to use me to put you two crime lords out of commission. I'm getting a key to the city after your trial."

"Hey, wait, let's calm down a second, guys," Von said. "Can't you see this whole dick caper thing is tearing us apart? This should be one of the happiest nights of our lives."

"Von's right," Greg said. "This is getting out of hand. I didn't really believe you had cops up there, Sammy. Sorry."

Von *hoped* he hadn't truly believed it, but he had his doubts. There was something more important than that, though. "And now that we've established that no one is trying to short-change no one else, what can you tell us about the attic, Sammy?" he asked.

"I can tell you you'll never see the inside of it if you don't make that phone call. Wait a second, though." He left the kitchen and returned a moment later with a cell phone. "Last one I grabbed had this on her, probably so she could call someone in the event of an emergency. Looks like she wasted her money, wouldn't you say?"

"It still works?"

Sammy handed it to Von, who saw the display was indeed lit up. "Hey, speaking of the recently abducted, we've got a present for you in the trunk, Sammy. Assuming she hasn't suffocated."

"Same thing happens to her either way," Sammy assured him. "She can wait."

Von punched in the Rochesters' number. "You boys ready to become millionaires?"

Greg looked more like he was ready to puke, but gave a thumbs up anyway.

Celia Rochester answered on the second ring. "Hello?"

"Good evening, Mrs. Rochester. Have you heard from your husband recently?"

"Do you know what time it is? If you're trying to sell me something, it's against the law to call this la—"

"Ma'am, I'm not trying to take your mon ..." Von stopped short. "I mean, I haven't broke the law ..." He stopped short again. "Look, this probably isn't what you think it is."

"Whatever it is, the answer is still the same. He's not here. He's away on business."

Von laughed. "Is that what he told you? I regret to inform you he was actually seen in the company of cheap women this evening at a local establishment called the Electra Complex."

Her voice turned hard. "Was he indeed?"

"Yes, ma'am, and—"

"That son of a bitch! That depraved, immoral, perverted little son of a bitch! He *promised* me never again!"

Her voice was now loud enough that Greg and Sammy could hear her clearly. Von held the receiver away from his head.

"Well, ma'am, I—"

"If he was here right now, you know what I'd do?"

"No, but—"

"I'd take a meat cleaver and chop him off. I'd dice his little cock into shish-kebab, that bastard—"

"In that case, I have some good news for you, ma'am. You see, we already took care of that for you."

"You diced it into shish-kebab?"

"Well, not exactly. It's still in one piece—" Here Von crossed his fingers. "—and if your husband wants it back, he's gonna have to pay us."

"Oh, he's not getting it back," she replied firmly. "He can spend the rest of his life pissing through a plastic tube for all I care."

The three men shared a look of absolute horror—not at the prospect of Edward Rochester pissing through a plastic tube for the rest of his life, but the increasing likelihood that there wasn't going to be any ransom payment.

"Wait, listen, the women really weren't that cheap, and he wasn't even buying lap dances, I swear!"

"Nice try, but I'm not going to be stupid about trusting my husband anymore."

"Okay, but what about compensation?"

"I'm not reporting you to the police. That's my final offer."

"We want our jillion dollars, you bitch!"

She hung up on him with an efficient little *click.*

"Well, Von, you ready to go buy that yacht now? Hell, let's go jet-setting," Sammy suggested, for once not enjoying his own sarcasm.

"It wasn't my fault," Von shouted.

"Wasn't it? All you had to do was say, 'Look, I cut off your husband's tool, and it'll cost you three million dollars to get it back so they can reattach it.' The way you did it, you may as well have said, 'Hey, your husband just raped a bunch of preschoolers after firebombing six hundred sixty-six churches and performing analingus on your mother's rotting cadaver, and by the way, how much will you pay to get back this penis I ripped from him?' If someone said they'd kidnapped your girlfriend while she was out slobbing knobs for a five-spot on Seymour and Laymon, would you pay up?" Von, who'd never actually had a girlfriend—not a willing one, at least—said nothing. He slammed the phone on the counter and curled his arm around the Tupperware bowl, almost protectively. He looked at the spoon, remembered its origin, and raised the bowl to his lips. He supped from it like it was the last of the milk in a cereal bowl.

"So you mean to say we ain't gettin' one red cent for what we've done tonight?" Greg asked.

"That's what I mean," Sammy clarified.

"You mean I had to put that guy's . . . that guy's *thing* in my mouth, and swallow it for nothin'?" Greg couldn't have looked more outraged if Movie Heaven stopped renting out *Gaping Anus.*

"Yep," Sammy agreed. "The eternal plight of women everywhere."

"Well, that's just low down as anything." He sulked, miserable at the idea that they probably *would* be shopping for yachts right now if Von had just read his script.

They were silent momentarily, stunned at this cruel turn of events, at a loss for words . . . the overconfident team who had boasted all along about their "inevitable" championship victory crusade, only to fall to the upstart underdogs. It wouldn't have seemed possible for their night to turn out worse than Rochester's, but here they were anyway. Every one of the involved parties, emasculated in one way or another.

As if on cue, they all heard a sudden outburst of laughter overhead which could only be construed as demonic. It did not seem to be predominantly masculine or feminine.

"Okay, I think we've had enough of your secrets," Von said. He about-faced and left the kitchen for the stairs, carrying the Tupperware bowl with him.

"It's safer if you don't go up," Sammy warned.

They ignored him. He tailed them with a sense of finality, not attempting to stop them. It was when they were passing

113

the door to the Divided Man that a voice froze them. "Look down here, boys. I want to see your faces before I paint the walls with your brains."

"Who's this B-movie actor?" Von asked Sammy as they all obeyed the directive. "Another one of your 'art' exhibits?"

They found themselves seeing all of Horace for the first time, not just the fresh stump of his manhood jetting haphazardly like a lawn sprinkler. He stood at the foot of the stairs, deathly pale, with the front of his jeans almost entirely soaked in blood. He held a .38 on them. "From my glove compartment," he explained. "I never drive without it. Guess I should have brought it inside the Electra Complex."

"I've never seen him before," Sammy replied to Von.

"Well, we don't recognize him either," Greg said.

"Of course you don't," Horace sympathized. "We weren't properly introduced before you ran off with my still-bleeding dick, now were we?"

"He ain't Edward Rochester," Greg said.

"Hell no he ain't," Von agreed. "The pale little son of a bitch is lying."

"Look at the front of my pants!" Horace shouted incredulously.

"*Homosexual* and pale," Von revised.

Sammy sighed. "Allow me to translate for you two jack-offs—you didn't castrate Rochester in the bar. Okay? You got *this* guy by mistake. Still with me? Now he's going to kill us all. The perfect end to the perfect night."

"Wrong guy? Bullshit." Von pointed at Horace. "Prove it."

Horace kept the gun on them while he undid the button of his jeans with his free hand and pulled his pants down. "You see now?" he asked triumphantly, then cried out when his underwear jostled the remnants. He had revealed something that looked more like a charred crater left by a meteorite than the external male reproductive system. His movements since the cauterization had teased open some of the heat blisters which had formed at the very base of his shaft (what little remained). Yellow pus was oozing over the rim of the blackened wound, the entrails of which were as indistinguishable as the remains of spontaneous combustion victims. The pus adhered to them like candle wax.

"Well then," Von said. "We stand corrected. But before you blow our brains out—" He heaved the contents of the Tupperware bowl in Horace's direction. They splattered across Horace's face, blinding him and—when he inadvertently swallowed some of them—sickening him. He covered his face with both hands, trying to clear his eyes.

The trio scrambled into the Divided Man's room and threw the door shut. Sammy had barely locked it and stepped back when the gun began firing on the other side, blowing out huge holes.

Von looked around frantically. "There's nothing here!" he said, referring to the lack of an arsenal. Greg gave the tube sock wide berth as he searched, also unsuccessful.

The gunshots destroyed the lock and Horace kicked the door open almost effortlessly and rushed in. Sammy collided with him immediately, slapping the gun loose. Sammy drove him over to the far wall where they both tripped over the Divided Man and collapsed beside the body. Nearest to them, Greg snatched Horace up by his hair and the belt of his pants and dragged him a few feet over. Greg set Horace face down in the chest cavity of Sammy's homage to *Gray's Anatomy*. Horace's face mashed the entrails flat and ripped some of the coils open. He inhaled the digestive juice remnants involuntarily, gagging as they burned his nostrils. They tasted even worse, he discovered a moment later, and he vomited explosively. At such proximity the bile washed along the inner walls like a gully, then rolled back under his face. He was dangerously close to drowning in his own vomitus when Greg let him go.

Horace jerked his head up, gasping and trying to wipe his face off with the front of his shirt. He closed one of his nostrils and exhaled through the other. A burning stream of gastric juice trickled out, like the fleeting last seconds of urination. He turned in time to see that Von had picked up his .38 from the floor and aimed it from a crouched position which left the gun poised at point-blank range in front of his already decimated crotch. Powder burns fanned across his thighs as the deafening blast of the gun evolved to a painful ringing sound in his ears.

Von attempted to punctuate by firing in Horace's screaming open mouth, but the gun was empty.

Horace wasn't finished. He'd already lost the main part of his anatomy, and the power sources were extraneous now anyway. He watched with an almost detached fascination as his testicles dropped out of either side of his pant legs. Von intentionally stepped on one, bursting it like an egg yolk as Horace shouldered past him and out the door in a seizure-like fashion.

Von and Greg helped Sammy up and followed the high-pitched screams. They caught up with him in the kitchen, just in time to see him snatch up the mallet Sammy had used to flatten Mary Jane Turner's anus. They cornered him, Sammy around the left side of the kitchen island and Von and Greg to the right.

Sammy ripped out a silverware drawer and removed a carving knife that wouldn't have shamed Michael Myers. His eyes never left Horace, who was backed up against the kitchen sink, head jerking left and right to plot a plan of attack.

Greg reached out to grab Horace's wrist. Horace yanked it away and swung the mallet on reflex. It struck a glancing blow across the crown of Greg's head with a hollow *thwock!* He stumbled backward and crashed into the corner of the room. He didn't move.

Von wisely backed away, scanning for a readily accessible weapon and finding nothing. He dropped to his knees as Horace swung for his head.

Aware that Sammy was right behind him, Horace pivoted and blindly lashed with the mallet. Sammy was just out of range, but the next mallet swing struck the knife and sent it clattering to the floor.

That was when Von reached up under Horace and grabbed a handful of his mangled crotch. Horace thought he felt something loosen and spurt, but he couldn't imagine what was possibly left to do so. Horace's vocal cords went taut as piano wire as he screamed, abruptly dropping the mallet.

Sammy seized it and swung it at Horace's head, putting his body into it. The mallet cracked loudly, with force brute enough to jar Horace's right eye from its socket. A dollop of blood sputtered over his cheekbone. The eyeball had not been freed; it was still connected by a straining optic nerve, and for the first time in his life Horace could see his face without a mirror. Von's hand was still wringing his crotch, and Horace kicked blindly behind him. He connected with something, and the hand was withdrawn.

Horace launched himself at Sammy, the momentum catching Sammy off-guard and putting him on his back with Horace atop. The mallet went down underneath his legs, just out of reach. Horace's eyeball dangled just above Sammy's face like a spider at the end of its web. His fingers were like talons, gouging at Sammy, seeking his eyes. The best Sammy could do was latch on to the wrists. He couldn't find the leverage to throw Horace off of him.

Finally, out of desperation, Sammy raised his head off the floor and opened his mouth. The hovering eyeball disappeared, and Sammy's teeth sprang shut like a trap. The optic nerve snapped and sprayed in his mouth. Horace immediately fell back from him, shrieking. Blood spurted between his fingers.

Sammy's head struck the kitchen floor and his teeth slammed shut again, this time on the actual eyeball. It burst like a salad tomato, filling up his mouth with ocular fluid. He got to one knee and spat the fragments in Horace's face.

"I'm not even the one who de-boned you," Sammy said.

Von was just picking up the Michael Myers knife when Sammy and Horace separated. He swung the knife overhead with both hands, plunging it into Horace's stomach as he fell on him. He sliced a six inch groove before the knife got stuck in the ribs. Horace screamed and jabbed a thumb in Von's eye. Von clapped a hand to his face, stumbling backward, crying out. Horace got to his unsteady feet, trying to withdraw the knife. He succeeded, but with the blade came the beginning ropes of his innards.

Horace kicked the mallet aside as Sammy got a hand on it, so Sammy snatched at the escaping coil at Horace's stomach. He narrowly missed a strike of the knife which Horace probably would have made had he been in possession of both his eyes. He couldn't adjust to the new depth perception. Sammy pulled the sticky ropes to the meat grinder and guided them through the slot, yanking another couple feet of intestine through the incision in the process. He started cranking the meat grinder like a tire jack. Skewered grayish clumps began piling up on the linoleum. Horace grabbed at the escaping coils in panic, trying to keep them inside, but they rolled through his fingers and fed themselves to the waiting teeth of the grinder. They were like the loose strings on a sweater which don't snap but continue to unravel the more you try to pull them and tear them off.

As a last resort, Horace cut his own entrails with the knife, which fortunately did not hurt. The internal hemorrhaging, on the other hand, was less merciful. Blood erupted from his nose and mouth. He stared with a kind of mute horror at the humiliation of his flesh.

Von tackled him from behind, slamming him into the kitchen sink. The unraveled length of intestine slapped wetly against the sink basin, curling through the lip of a black rubber cavity at the bottom. The knife bounced out of the sink and slid away on the counter until it struck the refrigerator.

"I've got him!" he called over his shoulder to Sammy. "Hit the switch!"

Horace bucked against him, but Von held on. Sharp elbows to his ribs and kicks to his shins started to loosen his grip, but then Sammy reached past and flipped the switch on an outlet beside the sink. The garbage disposal roared to life, the noise overpowering. Von worked Horace's hands behind his back, keeping him pushed up against the sink and away from the knife.

"Put it in!" Von tried to shout over the garbage disposal.

Sammy nodded with a little smile of amusement, as if to say, *Oh, this should be pretty neat.* He nudged the severed

118

length of bowel into the dark maw of the disposal drain until it poked through the hole in the rubber. It caught in the gears and pulled taut, now in a tug-of-war that Horace didn't look very likely to win. A spray of blood erupted from the drain in fine needlepoint spatters, like a reverse showerhead, painting Horace's face. Von used him as a shield to block the thrust of the backwash.

Horace made a final effort to free himself, still determined to take his tormentors with him if nothing else. He seized a handful of his entrails near the sink and wrenched at them. The rope of intestines tore apart. He tried to throw his weight in the direction of the knife, looking in that direction just in time to see the mallet whistling through the air. It cracked him above his remaining eye. Von let him drop to the floor, convulsing.

Sammy stood over him like a worker at the abattoir. He swung again. Six times. Twelve times. By twenty-four times, the blows ceased to register as anything solid and sounded more like large rocks striking the water of a creek bed. By thirty-three, Horace's own mother would have thought he was the Elephant Man. There were no further convulsions, only the persistent roar of the garbage disposal. Sammy finally flipped it off.

He and Von stood in contemplative silence.

Horace died bereft of dick, balls, right eyeball, right hand, and eighty percent of his internal organs.

"Hey, you forgot to paint the walls with our brains," Von informed the cadaver.

Greg groaned behind them, hauling himself back up to his feet by groping a shelf of the pantry. The throbbing pain was at least distracting him from the uprising of consumed genital remnants that seemed to have clogged his gullet.

"We better go get your slut out of the trunk just in case," Sammy said, as much to distract them from their original objective as to prevent further any surprises.

Minutes later they all stood in the moonlight behind the Nova. They could now hear Angelique pounding on the underside. Von popped the trunk and stood back.

119

A sweaty, gasping Angelique slid away from them as far as the trunk allowed, wrapped in fetal position.

"Look guys, I'm sorry for what I said earlier," she hyperventilated. "Just please don't hurt me. I'll do anything you want! I'll . . . I'll smoke with my box. I can do it with my asshole, too! Let me show you! F.O.C.!"

"Your butthole, eh?" Von said. "Sounds like it's our lucky night after all."

"Wait a minute," Greg said. "What *kind* of cigarettes? Cuz if it's just menthols, you can forget it."

Sammy addressed her as if the other two weren't even there. "You realize that doing '*anything*' we want could also easily lead to you being '*hurt*,' don't you?"

Von appraised him uneasily, practically seeing the perverse surgical configurations scrolling through Sammy's mind.

She raised a hand to them, as if to both ward them off and block out the sight of them altogether. "Please! My boyfriend's name is Edward Rochester, and he has a *lot* of money. He'll pay you for me . . . name your price! I have his number, just please don't hurt me!"

This brought them all up short. They exchanged looks and slowly began nodding.

Finally, Von spoke. "I say again, gentlemen: Are we ready to become millionaires?"

Part IV: Trading Pieces

Angelique didn't look particularly happy to be in Sammy's workshop, which may have had something to do with the duct tape holding her fast to the chair. It didn't help that Sammy was hovering over her, absently slapping his palm with a machete and grinning like the cat that ate the canary. He had also licked the length of the machete a few times, never taking his eyes from her. They took no chances with her, even wrapping her ankles fast to the chair legs. As a token medical measure for the cracked bone, they patched it with two strips in an X pattern (thus making it a target area if she somehow got free and tried to book . . . a kick in that place would put her right back to the ground in a hurry.)

She'd come up with what she felt were extremely convincing arguments for prolonging her life, but none of them actually got past the strip of tape over her lips. She may as well have been trying to recite the Gettysburg Address while deep throating Johnny Wadd.

Greg stood by the column of women dangling like slabs of beef from the overhead hooks. He ran his hands along each one like a housewife sizing up produce in a grocery store and gave their backsides a few hearty slaps.

"How'd you girls like to come home with a real man?" he asked.

He received a few whimpers by way of response, and a redhead (natural, he noted with no small satisfaction) pointlessly tried to explain that if Greg didn't call the police, Sammy was going to murder them all.

"Oh, well, that changes everything," Greg replied and laughed.

The protesting began anew.

Von winced. "What's the point of stealing 'em off the streets and raping 'em if you're just gonna let 'em nag like free women, Sammy? And why do you got her gagged when she should be calling Rochester and telling him to grab his checkbook?"

Sammy finally looked away from Angelique. "Don't tell me you bought her story."

"What do you mean?" Greg asked, then added, "Hey, Sammy, this girl ain't got no butthole."

"I *mean* think about it. Rochester's her boyfriend? Then why does he go to the Electra Complex and pay her forty bucks to hum him?"

Von frowned. "That's a good point. Hell, I wouldn't waste any of my money if I already had the prize. Wait a minute . . . did you say that girl didn't have a butthole?" He walked over to Greg, who was crouched beneath Mary Jane Turner's derriere. They both appraised the stringy crevice left over from Sammy's impromptu surgery like art aficionados in a museum.

"Impressive," Greg surmised.

"I've seen half dollars that were less rounded," Von said. Sammy beamed proudly.

"Hey, speaking of, how's that girl supposed to smoke with her asshole if we got her strapped down to that chair?" Greg asked.

Sammy sighed. "Will you give that up? It's not going to happen. Ever."

Greg sulked. "Well, that's just great."

"Cheer up. I'll find you a napkin before you go . . . make her do lipstick blots on it with her butt for you. Does that sound good to you?"

Greg grinned. "Best deal I had since Christmas."

"Hey, I want one too," Von said.

"Lipstick blots for all," Sammy affirmed.

"Hell, we don't have even a cigarette anyway," Greg pointed out.

"Anyway, it's not like you won't have your pick of butthole smokers when you get that cash," Von said.

"Oh, come on, Von!" Sammy shook his head. "Did you forget what we were just talking about? You know, you boys have a one track mind when it comes to ass . . . anyone's. I'm starting to worry about you. And she'd say anything to save *hers* right about now, don't you think? You got a better chance of Santy Clause giving you that money. Let's hear what other tall tales she's got bouncing around in her dicksucker, though . . . we'll liven up the night."

Sammy ripped the tape off Angelique's lips.

"You don't understand Rochester," she gasped. "He's really sick in the head. He gets off on paying me in the Vacuum. That's his kink, man! If he wasn't paying for it in a place like that, he wouldn't even care! He enjoys feeling like a pervert, like pure scum!"

"Well, I'm here to tell you the appeal of that wears off after about twenty-eight years," Von informed her. "There really ain't a whole hell of a lot of dignity left for me in pocket pussies and Rhonda Ream-Job dolls."

"I wouldn't know anything about that," Sammy

interjected, casting a wary eye toward Von, "but I definitely would have bought stock in motion lotion if I'd known I was going to wrack up so many solo frequent flyer miles."

"Damn, Sammy . . . why the hell are you jackin' down so much when you've got all these hot twats on tap down here?" Greg asked. "I don't get that at all."

"Unless 'hot twats on tap' is the answer why," Von speculated.

Sammy shrugged. "Sometimes if you want something done right, you've gotta do it yourself, especially when you can't pay to have it done. Which brings us back to the subject at hand."

"Let's give her a chance to prove herself," Von suggested. "It won't hurt anything if she's lying . . . except her, of course. Look at it this way, Angelique—you'll be saving lives. Most importantly your own. Do you think if we could afford to get laid that we'd be settling for deadhead fellatio?"

Angelique recoiled. "You're getting it from . . . *dead heads*? I only charge forty bucks at the Vacuum!"

Sammy shrugged again. "A machete only costs fourteen bucks. Comes with a sheath, too."

"You know how to get in touch with Rochester?" Von asked her.

"I have his cell phone number."

"Okay, so you'll call him and outline our terms. And don't try to tell him anything besides that."

"Yeah," Sammy added sarcastically, "definitely don't use your pre-arranged code phrase for 'I'm being held ransom in a basement with a bunch of naked women, including one with five extra vaginas and another with no asshole.'" Sammy gave Von a disgusted look.

"It pays to be careful," Von said defensively. "Why take the risk?"

"Why indeed? I'll make the call myself." He turned to Angelique. "If it's a wrong number, I'm going to work on you with a circular saw and iodized salt. This is your last chance to pull out." As if the same thing wouldn't happen to her regardless.

Angelique held her silence and only gulped audibly. If she'd known that amputation would only be the beginning of his overtures, the sound of her ass puckering up would have been audible through a bank vault. Sammy would never let someone die in such a passé fashion. For one, he would have mounted her as she lay there gushing blood from stumps at her elbows and knees, wallowing like a sea lion. He'd probably find the passage a bit dry, as sheer terror often had that effect on them, so he'd opt for plan B: the mouth. At this stage they generally thought they didn't have anything to lose, so biting would be their predictable attempt at a pathetic vengeance. That's when they found out they *did* have something left to lose, after all. Thirty-two somethings, as a matter of fact (if they'd brushed regularly). When the pliers came out, they'd do something Sammy wouldn't have believed possible of women if he hadn't seen it himself— they'd shut their mouths. Of course they'd eventually have to open them when Sammy pinched their nostrils shut, and then he'd prove a notorious adage—sometimes you really have to pull teeth if you want a woman to give you head. It took awhile to complete the excavation, and it wasn't too pretty to look at with all the gaps in their gums and a few dangling nerves besides, but it didn't take half the oxygen it would to blow up one of those dolls Von mentioned. He'd be soaked in blood like a newborn baby when he pulled out, but it wasn't that much different than laying down pipe in a girl during her monthlies. They wouldn't just bleed to death as Sammy poked and prodded for his standard thirty seconds, because he could tie off their severed arteries. Life assured that much longer, he'd been known to give the girls a hand— their own. One thrust between the legs, the other up the ass. Most would hemorrhage in the process of this internal handshake, but as they say, getting there is half the fun.

Naturally this wasn't his only option. He could do Angelique like Erica Granger (found 04/09/2002 under a NO DUMPING sign . . . and also throughout an elementary school playground and in a dumpster outside the police station). He'd raided his father's tackle box and fished out a few of those red and yellow plastic balls that bob in the lake when you get a bite. He'd secured several bait hooks to them with the help of adhesive so potent it would have removed his skin if he'd got any on his hands, and then strung the balls with fishing line.

Sammy didn't go out on the lake, though. He instead cast his makeshift reel into a prone Erica Granger's rectum, one ball after the other. He wore thick gloves and managed not to cut himself as he guided the custom-made anal beads deeper within. She was squirming in unadulterated agony long before he prodded the fourth one home, so all that protruded was a few inches of fishing line, which he twirled around his finger like dental floss. She looked like one of those talking dolls with a cord in the back, though in this case each yank was another scream. It took more effort than he expected to jerk them free. He'd make a few inches of progress and then the hooks would catch on something more resistant in her digestive tract. It was like trying to run through sticker bushes dragging a parachute. He was too mesmerized by the tiny tearing sounds and the emerging hooks—dragging yellow and purple strands and clumps—to even notice that Erica had died somewhere between the removal of the second and third ball. It was for this gross insolence that she was humiliated when it came time to dispose of the body. They found one section of her cadaver from waist to thighs with an added bonus—her head secured between her legs with ten-penny nails, tongue staple-gunned to her vulva.

It would almost be worth the loss of his chance at a six figure income to work similar magic on Angelique.

"Sammy?" Von brought him back to reality.

"Eh? Oh, yeah . . . the phone." Sammy punched in the number Angelique gave him.

A man answered, sounding rather infuriated. "Yes?"

"Is this Edward Rochester?"

"Who's this?"

"I'm the guy asking the questions. Are you Rochester?"

"I am."

Sammy raised a thumb. Von and Greg brightened like

kids waking up on Christmas morning. Sammy turned his back on them so he wouldn't be sickened and placed a hand on Angelique's shoulder to steady himself.

"Okay," he continued. "I believe you've made the acquaintance of a certain Angelique?"

"That would not be incorrect."

"Great, then we have something in common."

"What's this about? Are you trying to blackmail me?"

"No, although five minutes from now you're probably going to wish that's all it was."

"Maybe I will, if you actually manage to get to the point by then."

"I'll give you the condensed version. I've got Angelique, and I'm offering you the opportunity to buy her back for three million dollars. If you say yes, I'll give you further instruction. Assuming everything goes smoothly, you'll get her back good as new. If you say no, I'll do a job on her that would make the attractions at a freak show puke their guts."

"I see. And will you throw in my dick at half price if I act now?"

"I didn't make that call to your wife, although in all fairness to my associates, they thought that the one in their possession came from you. It was an honest mistake that anyone could have made." Not liking Rochester's smart-ass method of negotiating, Sammy attempted to get a little rise out of him. "Your wife wasn't disturbed in the least, by the way."

"No, she wouldn't be. It was a different story when she found out I was unharmed."

It wasn't the reaction Sammy had hoped for, but he wasn't exactly surprised. There was more than one way to skin a twat, though, as they said (or at least he did). He made no reply to Rochester and merely held the phone to Angelique's head. "Talk," he commanded.

"Eddie, please *help!* They've got all these women down here to torture them and they want me . . . they want me to . . . to smoke with ..." Here her convincing plea dissolved into incomprehensible histrionics as panicked sobs overtook her. If he'd draped a paper bag over her head, she probably would have gasped a hole through it.

Sammy removed the phone from her ear and brought it to his own "You still think we're playing a game, Henny Youngman?"

"No," Rochester said after a moment of silence.

"Well, you were right the first time; it *is* a game. Just not the kind your little *bitch* can afford to lose. Now then, did I get to the point fast enough for you? Welcome to the next level, mother*fucker*."

"Has she been hurt?" Finally, some actual concern.

"She broke a bone in transit, but she'll live to suck another day."

"I want to think about it."

"She's not a used car, Ed. She's a D-cup brunette with an ass that won't quit—"

But allegedly would smoke, *under the right circumstances*, he thought.

"—unless we don't get our three million dollars. No more glory hole loads down the hatch, at least not from you. There'll be thousands from us before we put her pretty little ass outta biz, though, you can bet on that. And probably *millions* more after that."

A white lie . . . *Sammy* would have thousands and millions more, yes. Von and Greg would be outta luck *and* outta biz, though. His basement, his rules.

"So think about that as you mull it over—" Sammy reached for an adequate insult and remembered something Von said earlier. "*Fag face.* You have twenty minutes." Sammy ended the call and then turned it off altogether for the time being. It was unlikely anybody would be attempting to triangulate its position so soon, but as Von said, it pays to be careful. It might pay three million dollars.

He turned to relay the news to the dysfunctional duo.

"*Shiiiiiiiit,*" he said, clenching the phone in his hand hard enough to dislodge the back cover and send it clattering to the concrete.

They were gone.

***

The instant Sammy's back was turned, Greg and Von crept up the stairs at Von's behest. They could find out later what came of the phone call, but this might be the only unescorted chance they got tonight at the attic. Once clear of the basement, Von stealthily eased the door shut and then they were through the kitchen and up the stairs like a shot, all but trampling one another on the last flight. Even now they could hear the faint, strange laughter which had tantalized them throughout the evening.

Sammy's secret.

"If it's Slut Necro Lambda's twin sister, I got dibs on that backdoor," Greg proclaimed.

"Hell with that," Von said promptly, elbowing his cohort to all fours. He reached the top of the dim corridor first, although he was prevented from going in when Greg clamped his arms around his legs.

"If I didn't know better, I'd think you were hugging me," Von said. "I'm tempted to drop-kick your ass down the stairs anyway. Have you lost your mind? We don't have much time before Sammy realizes we're gone."

Greg reluctantly withdrew and hauled himself to his feet. Von tried the door.

"Locked," he reported glumly. He stared the door down defiantly. "You son of a whore."

"Cussin' it ain't gonna help," Greg said.

"Eat a dick," Von replied absently, then remembered. "Another one, I mean."

Greg shoved him. "Why don't you grab you another one through a glory hole?"

Von ignored him. "Question is, do we break it down? He may have a good reason to lock it up. This could turn into a huge problem that we don't need tonight."

"But what if he's only locking it cause it's his best work and he's too selfish to share it with us?"

"That *would* be pretty low of him," Von concurred, conveniently forgetting about how they never invited Sammy to take a ride on that body they found on the road awhile back or share in any of the spoils of Geisha Hammond, or how they'd had every intention of not only cheating Sammy out of millions of dollars but possibly *killing* him to have it all to themselves.

"And he could have dead guys stashed all over the house that we don't know about. What if he stitched 'em together to create some kind of superman to guard the door if we ever came back?"

"Let's break it," Von said immediately. Sammy obviously couldn't surgically create some kind of superhuman sentinel like Greg was worried about (at least Von didn't *think* he could), but he *would* do something to make it more difficult for anybody to get in now that he knew someone was determined to see inside. It was now or never. Anything *too* crazy would need a little more than just a door to keep it in place, wouldn't it? This had to be something too good to share.

They both reared back and kicked above the door knob the way the cops did on TV, managing to do so mostly in synch for the next few attempts. The door finally splintered and swung inward on the fifth try.

Von entered the attic first, feeling for a light switch in the total darkness. There were no windows and no hint of light anywhere. They stumbled in blindly, fully expecting to run into or fall over something. Von flinched when something touched his face, but a moment later he identified it as the chain from an overhead bulb. He yanked it and recoiled when something in the corner of the attic simultaneously shrank back from the light.

"Who are they?" a woman's voice said.

"Who's she talking to?" Greg asked, alarmed, looking around.

"She talks to them," the woman explained.

"*She* is a few bullets shy of a clip," Von noted.

She emerged from the darkened corner for a better look at them, squinting into the light like someone emerging from a mine shaft. She propelled herself with her arms, dragging

129

her legs behind her like they were as useless as a mermaid's fins on dry land.

"What happened to her legs?" Greg asked, as if Von had read her medical file.

"Looks like she was in a fire."

Von was no doctor, however, so it was no surprise that he confused burn marks with tertiary syphilis. Perhaps there was a vague resemblance. There did appear to be several patches along her hips and thighs where a couple layers of flesh had been scorched away, and in some instances they looked to have decomposed to stages of adipocere. They resembled fatty deposits of custard which had crusted in mounds to her skin. Von suddenly found himself thinking of a cheese pizza he'd heated in an oven for way too long.

Her hair was stringy and wild, obviously unwashed for days; maybe months. She dragged a sizable belly along the floor with her, like a dachshund. Her sagging breasts had what Von liked to call Oscar Meyer nipples, so large he just wanted to lop them off with a cleaver and toss them between two slices of bread. Where there weren't nipples, there were enough blue lines to chart the rivers in a map of Alaska.

"They aren't supposed to be here," she announced. "She's not supposed to see them. She's not for their eyes. She's—"

"She's about to get raped, son!" Greg supplied for her.

"Amen to that," Von agreed. "I don't care if she didn't have better sense than to park her ass on a wood-stove . . . I'm gonna blast my load so far up that joyhole they'll have to wring out her kidneys to get a sperm sample."

"She'll bite him," she warned.

"Then she'll have to be beaten unconscious first. You do the honors, Greg."

Greg nodded, mistakenly thinking that Von would give him first crack at her box if he corralled her. It wouldn't have mattered either way. She pounced on Greg without warning, and were Von not carrying one dandy of a hard-on in his jeans, he would have laughed. He was far more interested in tenderizing some bone dry beaver than seeing Greg embarrass himself yet again, though, so he was mostly just aggravated.

"Von, get her off me! She's using her teeth! Please, Von, she might have AIDS! C'mon, let's just bang her and get the hell out of here!"

"Keep her occupied!" Von then unleashed the beast and set its course for Gash City. He certainly didn't prefer to feel the deformities on her posterior, but he didn't have all night to question the aesthetics. Sammy wouldn't stay occupied forever, and truthfully Von couldn't care less if Greg got his turn at bat. It was too bad for him, though, because he was definitely missing out. The passage to pleasure wasn't without some moisture, although not immediately. It was more like there were mild obstructions as Von thrust for maximum depth, but his friction managed to puncture them and drain whatever juices they contained. It was easier going soon enough . . . if he tried not to think about all those runny scab-like things he was sliding against. He couldn't decide if the squishing sounds were from his entry or those burn wounds peeling away and oozing. As the woman thrashed violently to free herself from either Greg or Von, he decided he didn't much care. Either way, she was going to have some extra grease on the skillet in about 2.2 seconds.

He exploded enough to fill a two-pint milk carton just seconds before Sammy's determined footsteps reached the attic stairs. He reluctantly pulled out and hurriedly reassembled his pants, though it was hard not to be distracted by her legs—the algae-like manifestations were positively *seeping* now, the semen-like emissions spreading down to her heels.

Von was pulling up his zipper when Sammy burst in, none too happy.

"What are you doing with my mother?" he asked.

"Tell the man, Greg," Von said, craftily implying an accusation.

"Sammy, just get her off me, please!"

"They meant to rape her!" Sammy's mother proclaimed. "He already did!"

"I'd have thought you'd learn your lesson by now," Sammy said to Greg.

"*Me?* But I—"

"Short of cutting off my own or Von's—" Von flinched. "—I can't rustle up another dick for you to chew on. Except yours, maybe."

"But I—"

"But no, I wouldn't do that. I understand the temptation all too well." Sammy fondly cupped his mother's breast. She smiled at him, and lasciviously licked her lips. "It's been my burden to live with her this way four years now. Her excesses resulted in the premature germs of insanity . . . her vices sprang up fast and rank. I could never put her away, though, not when we're so close."

He slowly pulled her off Greg and gently set her down beside him. "I told you not to come up to the attic, though, for this very reason."

"She bit me," Greg complained, looking rather faint. He attempted to get up.

Sammy firmly planted a foot on his chest. "Look what you've done to her legs."

"But I—"

"I'm a big believer in putting things back the way you found them, so I'm going to nicely ask that you lick her clean. Then all will be forgiven."

"Don't do the crime if you can't do the time," Von admonished. "Lock and load."

Greg looked at the slick, crusty terrain with mortal terror. Somehow the thought of eating the aborted remnants from the refrigerator seemed preferable to this. He felt like pointing out that he wasn't completely responsible for the damage, but one look at Sammy's face revealed there would be no bargaining. Greg winced painfully, extended his tongue, and maneuvered his face over the mother's heels. He closed his eyes and descended until his tongue met the skin. His taste buds seemed to wither on contact like time lapse photography, but he forced himself further up, bathing her like a cat. The flavor was hideous, damn near unspeakable. He thought of a carton of orange juice, where the final swallows are enriched by a multitude of dregs, only this taste was not of citrus but spoiled honey mustard . . . which it looked like, too.

"She could get use to this," the mother said.

The actual fluids were nothing compared to the boils and pustules from which they emitted. Their flaky, encrusted textures—like nipples still smoking after a few jolts from a Die Hard battery—were almost Greg's swan song. He wanted to die then, to never see another day. He was crying again for the second time that night as he finished.

Sammy searched the mostly bare floor a moment before he found a drinking cup his mother had used for months. He removed the straw from it and handed it to Von.

"While I call Rochester, you get on all fours and retrieve that load you shot in my mother before I got up here."

Von's jaw hit the floor. He accepted the straw dumbly.

"Lock and load," Greg mocked. He promptly gagged and puked into a silhouetted corner of the attic.

Sammy made the phone call as Von guided the straw into a place that just moments ago he'd been rather fond. He uncertainly put his lips at the end and tried to summon the courage.

"You made up your mind?" Sammy asked when Edward Rochester picked up.

"Yes . . . I've decided to pass. Do whatever the hell you want with her. I've got four more like her at the Electra Complex alone."

Von sucked and was mortified to vividly see the ejaculate ooze back to him, like some kind of horror movie in reverse. A vein stood out in his forehead from the effort. It was one of those ridiculous straws with all the spirals, something he could remember vividly from childhood and hadn't thought of in ages. His progress was slow and hard-fought. It felt like he was drinking a milkshake through a coffee straw.

Sammy was silent a moment. "I strongly recommend you reconsider."

Greg, who had stopped crying, looked on the verge of a reprisal when he understood Rochester wasn't going to pay up. Von was too absorbed by his own misery to notice. The first sips of his recon mission had arrived, and he instantly spat them onto the floorboards. When he discovered the salty discharge wasn't purely white, he very much wanted to die just like his cohort.

"There's nothing for me to reconsider," Rochester said to Sammy, "but I have a proposition that might interest you."

Celia Rochester awoke from uneasy dreams to discover she was no longer herself. Nor was she in her own bed. She was in a basement, flat on her back beneath bright fluorescent lights. She could not remember how she got here, but that seemed somewhat less important than how she wound up with two new breasts sewn beneath the ones she was born with, or why maggots were busily writhing in and around an anus which had certainly not been in her belly when she was last conscious.

"They fight off infection," Sammy explained.

Von stood to the side cradling a disembodied head. "Poor Angelique," he said. "She knew so well . . . fellatio." He unzipped his pants. Noticing Celia's baffled look, he said, "Hey, I might be a millionaire, but if I can save forty bucks, why not? Way I see it, your husband's the sick one." The back of Angelique's head was soon gliding to and fro.

Celia tried to scream, but generated no sound at all.

"Edward told us to remove your vocal cords, though I don't think he expected you to survive the procedure. He of little faith." Sammy shrugged. "Ever seen emphysema put a hole in someone's throat? I took the liberty of giving you one . . . except I transplanted a certain stripper's vagina to spice it up. You might say we have a grand new opening."

Greg appeared beside her and began pawing her breasts. All four of them. Two for the discriminating breast connoisseur who could not abide by any artificial embellishment—these were Celia's own—and two more paid for by the generous "philanthropists" of glory hole transactions in the Vacuum, silicone deposits which Angelique obviously had no use for anymore.

This was the life.

Rochester stowed the payment away in the trunk of

Celia's car with the option for Sammy, Greg, and Von to grab her anywhere they wanted (coincidentally they got her at an underground parking garage on her way to a divorce lawyer's office). It made it that much easier to ensure that they got back to Sammy's "laboratory" without any fear of being followed to home base, something that might have otherwise been problematic if Rochester had any emotional involvement to the "package."

Three million dollars was a very good start, and it is most surely a victory when you can get paid for doing what you love.

And they were thinking about doing it to the eight other Saturday night dancers from the Electra Complex, four of whom were adamant that a certain Edward Rochester would pay dearly for their safety.

It might not result in any financial advantage, but a sister for Slut Necro Lambda was surely a worthy endeavor regardless. Getting there would be half the fun and a lot more besides.

It was worth a try.

FINAL INDICATIONS

Section I

This was never written. You are not reading this sentence. None of the following ever happened.

It's after the end of the world . . . don't you know that yet?

Anything that is said to have happened after December 31, 1999 is an illusion; a stubborn reflection from smoke and mirrors in the midst of a vast cosmic emptiness. I didn't see it this way at first. I clearly recall waking up on the day masquerading as January 1, 2000. A day like any other, except it really wasn't. Its arrival was one of the anticipated question marks in history, although there was nothing to indicate this in the headlines I saw on the newsstand. HAPPY NEW YEAR! was the best some of them could do.

The final seconds of December didn't tick by so much as wind down, and it had to cross everyone's mind that maybe we were spinning on the axis of a global tomb. We were privileged to be the children of millennial paranoia, and we dutifully watched the skies and waited for the great infernos.

Nothing happened.

"Ah . . . knew it all along" rapidly replaced the more uneasy sentiment of "We may be dicked" from twenty-four hours before. No one has ever been as disappointed as I was when I found myself earthbound at 12:01 a.m. I was so numb you could have performed open heart surgery on me without anesthesia. I'd wanted total death for everyone and everything, the entire creation laid in ashes. No great advances in humanity, no new breakthrough by which to measure our unremarkable evolution, no more accolades for reinventing the wheel. This wasn't an idle hope for me. I'd *felt* it, like a pregnant woman feeling her baby kicking; a glorious certainty.

It was in the trepidation we all felt standing in line at the post office, watching those digital clocks with the red numbers running backward (310 DAYS 17 HOURS 26 MINUTES 32 SECONDS . . . 31 SECONDS . . . 30 SECONDS . . . until 2000). The smiles were too long, the laughter too forced, the desperate glances too apparent. The cancer was awake in us all, and nothing was benign anymore. . . . But nothing happened.

The heavens did not open, and renegade angels did not begin tear-assing through the skies to lay waste with fire and brimstone. Extraterrestrials didn't glide in on flying saucers and eradicate an experiment gone awry. Warheads didn't rocket into the most populated cities and burn everyone to radioactive embers. The old people who lived below me read aloud from the Book of Revelation, as if it were an incantation to summon their lord.

No one came. No one left. I spent most of New Year's Day waiting for the impetus to go ahead and end it all, but like the storm of Armageddon I'd eagerly awaited throughout 1999, it never came. Perversely, the time did not feel right for even that just yet. I was resigned to continue. Supposedly a year away from inhabitable space stations and homicidal computers named HAL, we were still mastering the art of cracking skulls by the watering hole. In the interim, years passed, always with this sense that we had let a golden opportunity slip away, our best chance at world incineration forever lost.

And what I saw was worse than I'd imagined. A new era without a substantial revelation was a sobering concept, but I wasn't prepared for its actuality. Everyone was embracing the end of innovation. It didn't matter to them that everything

137

had been done before. It could be overcome, they reasoned, by exhaustive repetition. The sterility of the radio reached a new low. Lifeless three minute sound bytes were the hymns of choice in the secret praise of creative impotency. In theaters, everything was a remake, a sequel, or an adaptation of an old TV show. Books were streamlined to pull us to the end more quickly; plot and characters were incidental. The mediums we used to put our pointless lives aside were corrupted. No aesthetic and no catharsis. Even language had become infantile—phrases like the *C word, N word, R word, F bomb*, a watchdog society taking on the role of that kid in first grade who couldn't wait to tell the teacher you said a bad word like "shut up."

Social networking, too. A world more in contact with each other than ever, and we chose to tell each other what we ordered for lunch.

I was forced to seek solace in my work. My job had always been a somewhat amusing distraction before, but now I was asking it to carry all the weight. The endeavor was unquestionably doomed, but there was simply nowhere else to turn. I was on the outskirts of the Information Age. I wrote the text to those pamphlets you find in doctor's offices, insurance agencies, college campuses and the like. Very inspirational stuff with titles such as *First Indications of Trichomoniasis* and *Do You Have Ovarian Cancer?* I spent forty hours a week writing condensed prophecies of suffering for people who hoped against hope their symptoms were anything but. I warned students that unprotected sex was that first step on the road to painful sensations while urinating and the ultimate failure of the immune system. My office was adorned with a sign reading DON'T BLAME THE MESSENGER.

I developed a new fascination with my subject matter. Diseases were rather admirable. Once they realized they could be cured, they mutated. Sickness was the only source of originality anymore. The way it took control of you was essentially a form of possession. It altered your physiology and psychology, as well as how you were perceived by those around you. Your proximity became unbearable. Contagious, too, possibly; if not then, a few generations down the bloodline when the genetic remnants chose to activate, like a bomb hurled through the portal of a time machine. I wasn't being asked to discourse on the skillful adaptation of diseases, however, and that eventually cost me my obsession. I was another cog to keep the post-1900s repetition machine rolling. Each pamphlet was more of the same: *Because you failed to wear one of these or you ate too much of this or you have too little of that, you are going to feel marginal discomfort, suffer greatly, or consider contacting a lawyer about making out your last will and testament. The following procedures might increase the rather futile chances of your recovery, or prolong your pain beyond all sanity.* Words like "agony" and "death" lost all meaning to me; they were just 12-point letters in a universal font on my screen.

When I abandoned all hope and interest, Ursula came into my life. The artist who had always drawn the anatomical diagrams for the pamphlets moved on. His big break had apparently come when his highly original comic strip featuring the daily "hilarities" in the life of a nuclear family was optioned for nation-wide syndication. Our man Murphy had drawn his last rendering of fallopian tubes and sauntered over to greener pastures. He didn't bow out with much notice, so we needed a verrucose urethra in a bad way. I think they accepted the first person to apply, and it turned out to be her.

"Hello, I'm Ursula," she said by way of introduction. She was very stiff-postured, and her handshake would have made rigor mortis envious. She gave off no genuine warmth, and I think that's what attracted me to her. I saw myself mirrored in her lack of enthusiasm. The women I generally worked with were perky types who would probably be wowed by flowers and stuffed animals. Ursula didn't seem the type to ally herself with them, and seemed embarrassed for them.

I introduced myself and gave her the text for the pamphlet. I had to test her; had to know immediately. "At one point," I said, "there was talk of using diagram templates instead of just having an artist. I don't know what came of that."

Ursula showed no visible reaction. "There are too many templates already, don't you think? Just the same sources waiting to be dressed up a little, if at all."

Her answer told me more than I'd been seeking. She'd echoed me even more strongly.

"When are you going to lunch?" I asked. Things began to evolve from there. I could give a synopsis of our conversation that day and not even have to tell you who said what. The answers would have been the same for either of us.

"What are your career goals?"

"I have none."

"How do you feel about violence?"

"Quite good."

"Do you foresee better things for the world in general next year?"

"Quite the opposite."

And so on. We only deviated from this when I asked about her artistic talent. She said, "That's a gray area. I think my work—what I do for myself—is becoming something very different."

Something stirred in me. I immediately sensed she didn't mean "different" as in different for her. There was an uncertainty in her voice tinged with hope, like that of an astronomer who believes he has discovered a new planet. I don't know why I was inspired at all. The bases had to have been covered, from etchings on cave walls and pyramids to portraits, landscapes, images of Hell and soup cans. From stone to canvas to hologram. What was left to be different? Collective unconscious is a rather limiting concept.

But I *was* inspired, as I hadn't been since my premonitions of 1999. I was no artist myself. I'd liked comics before they became less about mythologies and more about foil, gold, and holographic covers (I'd been so into *The Uncanny X-Men* in sixth grade that I demanded to know why adamantium wasn't on the Periodic Table), but about the only character I could draw was one with the power of eternal invisibility. My masterpiece was a stickman rendering of Charles Whitman sniping students from the observatory tower. I felt like I had a real vision, but I wasn't convinced that more talent would be enough to express it. I'd never considered a conduit before.

Section II

When I met Ursula, the signs returned almost instantly. They were like images congealing in a haze of static. Words seeping through my apartment walls from a neighbor's stereo: *I'll make you yearn for the Apocalypse.* A fragment of dialogue from the TV: *There's no tomorrow. You know why? It ain't ever gonna get here!* Cryptic abbreviations carved on walls in benches and bathrooms suggesting more than so and so was here or so and so gives a great ream: Axxon N, Z2K, EOTA.

Something was awake under the surface of things, something with a lot more momentum than another self-proclaimed reincarnation of Christ stockpiling assault rifles or pouring Kool-Aid. Ursula knew I sensed it, but I didn't try to express it. I wasn't sure I could. What I did talk about was sickness and my respect for its innovation. Even this wasn't without its merits, as I generally couldn't talk about Hansen's disease over pastrami sandwiches and chicken salad with anyone. Ursula would hint at new art she was excited about, but she never elaborated. I doubted she was the type who believed that talking about an incomplete project would somehow compromise it, but I didn't press her. I didn't want to hear I was wrong about the significance of her work—a possibility I couldn't ignore, not after the disappointment of January 1, 2000. It wasn't until after another New Year's that she said, "There are some people I really think you should meet."

Section III

They had a studio on Bava Lane, "they" being Ursula, Lee, Geoff, and Rebecca. This came to three more people than I ever would have guessed Ursula could work with, but there was an unmistakable synergy among them. It was more akin to the type you'd find in a back room where terrorists were hatching a bombing than the origin of substantial art, so I fit right in.

"We all attended Kinion University," Ursula explained. "Slightly different capacities, but somehow we got together. I had a still life course with Geoff."

Geoff looked like an artist, and a starving one at that. Wiry thin with long black hair and an apparent love of caffeine, judging by his inability to stay still (I bet he'd done rather poorly in the class with Ursula). He nodded at this introduction, and disappeared behind a canvas.

Lee waited for no cue. He stepped forward with an imposing mass and a shirt with the letters EOTA. "I'm Lee," he said. "And I shape the revelations." One of the hands that did so swallowed mine in greeting. Behind him was something that looked like a torso in progress, which seemed strange because there didn't appear to be any clay left to build onto it. Beside him was a human-sized structure covered with a white sheet.

Rebecca did not seem to realize there was anyone else in the world, much less the studio. She sat cross-legged on a chair, poised over a notebook, scribbling furiously and then crossing out just as aggressively. "Our resident poet Rebecca," Ursula said, gesturing. Rebecca did not acknowledge hearing her name. Ursula quietly added, "I met her in an ethics class. The professor failed her for not sleeping with him."

"And you passed," Rebecca finally said, still not looking up. "Irony is an art form unto itself."

Rebecca had no response for this, but the scribbling grew more animated. I looked to each of them, wondering. A very unlikely assembly line of profundity. I was a step away from disenchantment when another message reached me from a CD player off in the corner—*The world you see around you is just an illusion.*

I turned to Ursula. "What's all this really about? You didn't bring me here to preview an art exhibit."

"None of this is for show," she replied stiffly. I certainly hoped not, because there wasn't much of one to see. I'd seen the back of a canvas, a glum poet, a demented sculptor, and precious little else. Disorder prevailed from wall to wall in the debris of discarded canvases, knives, random droplets of paint, used palettes, a welder's mask, blowtorch, scrap metal, and various odds and ends. Somehow I didn't think the historical society would intervene if the city decided to raze the building.

"So what's it for?" I challenged. I wanted to know there was an objective that had never been carried out before. There *had* to be. I couldn't seamlessly go back to summarizing the effects of chlamydia in fifteen hours. I wanted to leave with a purpose.

"It's ready," Geoff said from behind his canvas. "I'll show him."

"You're sure he's going to be okay?" Lee asked Ursula, meaning me. He didn't sound overly concerned that I might not be.

"Show him," Ursula said.

Geoff stepped back out from the canvas, hands shaking from either excitement or twelve cups of coffee. He approached Rebecca, who finally looked up to reveal emerald eyes that Geoff or Ursula should have been painting. He extended his vibrating hand and clenched it just above her head. There was a sound like paper tearing, and he yanked his hand aside. Where Rebecca had been sitting suddenly tore apart from the fabric of reality and fluttered to the ground. The back of the shredded scenery was an unblemished white. A foreboding black gulf had revealed above it. The edges wavered as though blown by a wind within the resulting abyss.

Geoff knelt and picked up the fallen sheet. The bottom was still attached to the floor, every bit as real. Of course, who was to say just how much of what I was seeing did in fact exist? Geoff held up the page that moments ago had been a determined if not exactly socially adventurous poet. She was still there, but no longer mobile. To look at her you wouldn't have known she was animated before. What I was seeing now was just a poster.

"How do you bring her back?" I finally asked, after a heavy silence.

"Back from where?" Lee countered. "She never existed."

"And I didn't pass that ethics class," Ursula said.

Geoff turned his canvas where I could see it. The painting depicted an otherwise unremarkable interpretation of the near wall of the studio . . . except in the middle of it there was a black space with ripped edges.

Section IV

They could have brought Rebecca back, but she was only three dimensional in the visual sense. Her personality was at best two dimensional, a conglomeration of her creators' traits: Lee's sarcasm, Ursula's interest in poetry, and Geoff's relentless work ethic and revision fetish. As such, she was probably better off in whatever purgatory she'd been cast in.

"We call it the Golem Phenomenon," Ursula said. "Traditionally the monster known as the golem kills the one who used magic to create it. There's a great metaphor for the plight of the artist in that myth; so often the artist ahead of his or her time suffers for any innovation."

"Condemned," Geoff agreed.

"His value is assessed by a wide audience often incapable of objectivity."

"Or thought," Lee added.

"It's a blasphemy in our eyes that it should be this way. Those with the need to create are basically used and discarded according to the prejudices and limitations of the only people they can show their work. We certainly weren't looking for this to change. There didn't seem to be any way around it. But the funny thing is that there *was* a way."

I was thinking all this philosophizing was abstract, and there were certainly no stones left unturned in abstraction. Then Lee proved me wrong.

"Simply put, the world ended."

Section V

This was never written. You are not reading this sentence. None of the following ever happened.

Section VI

Their theory was madness, and before January 1st of our new epoch, I never would have put any credence in it. What if there wasn't a 2000, though? No act of inhumanity could allow the proper alignments for the end process. The twentieth century saw the merciless execution of millions in war, mostly by-standers . . . then came the birth of rock 'n roll, and everything was okay again. Maybe as long as we were being fairly inventive about our methods of mass destruction, we preserved ourselves. What if even that ran out, though? What if the repetition and stagnation of art was mirrored not only in the boring cultures it portrayed but its cutting edge science as well? What if said scientific breakthroughs were just experiments in *cloning?* Did it not signify something when the sum of our advances stopped being half as fantastic as the dreams of artists, and the artists' dreams themselves stopped being all that impressive?

Why had I really thought I would know the shape of the end? With such ambition and on such a grand scale, would it not have to be something previously unseen and unforeseen?

Section VII

"Think starlight," Ursula said. "By the time it gets to us, it's thousands of years old. Those stars could be dead, but you'd never know it to look at the night sky. We'll think they're alive for millennia after they've burnt out."

Lee smirked. "Now there's a fresh metaphor for you."

Geoff said, "Personally, I think you're wasting your time trying to convince him that way. The important thing is that a woman who never existed before was very alive before we ripped her from our reality like a page in a notebook.

We believe this wasn't something anyone could do before the end of the century. Something shifted in the relationship between art and its limits, maybe because it *had* to."

Ursula wasn't about to be denied another metaphor. "If you accept the idea that the universe was a clock wound and abandoned by a creator, what happens in the time between when it is stopping and rewound? Maybe something new. We felt it. This wasn't something we accidentally discovered. We *knew* it would work. We weren't waiting for the right time, but *no* time. That's where we are now. Artists all over the world could interpret the same subject to no effect, but when the three of us do it, it *lives.*"

Section VIII

The trial and error behind this had been the cause of its obscurity. It was not the kind of thing they wanted to publicly experiment with, because they could not afford any attention before mastery. To do what they'd just done with Rebecca . . . to make her exactly as they wanted . . . wasn't innate. (I can't say it took *time* to learn, because by that point there was no longer any such thing.) Their ideology valued art over humanity, and in their hands art was no idle expression awaiting admiration, condemnation, or indifference. Their golems were still hostile, but not toward the authors. It was the audience endangered now. Don't blame the messenger; kill the recipients. I was like-minded, but that didn't explain why Ursula wanted me there. The why behind their new talent was of secondary importance to me anyway; I wanted to know *what.* What could be done with it? And *how.* How far could it go?

"Want to try an experiment?" Geoff asked.

Section IX

If somewhere there is a race of almond-eyed extra-terrestrials bending time and space to travel great distances and dislocate the rectums of unlucky homo sapiens with their excruciating

146

probes, perhaps they will land on this planet long after it is deserted and wonder where all the potential rape victims absconded. Maybe they will sift through the ruins to find clues to the great exodus. This would be the first.

From *The Herald,* article by Jackson Zirnheld.

"MAN CLAIMS ASSAULT BY ANIMATED VILLAIN"

While walking home from work, Peter Swaggerty was undeniably attacked. Beyond that, the facts are difficult to establish. Swaggerty insists that his broken limbs and extensive bruising resulted from the assault of a figure he claimed was an animated drawing.

"Sure, I know it sounds crazy," he concedes, "but I know what I saw. It was like some kind of insane dream that I still haven't woken up from." He describes his assailant as "sleek and very powerful. We've all seen him for years on those old neighborhood watch signs, the guy who's a black silhouette except for his crazy eyes. He's the one who attacked me last night, as if he stepped right off the sign to pummel me. He looks like that Marvin the Martian cartoon in his face, but Marvin the Martian never said stuff like 'I'm gonna pull your entrails right through your [backside].'"

Swaggerty suffered six cracked ribs, eight broken fingers, elaborate facial damage, a dislocated shoulder, a compound ulnar fracture, and two broken legs as he attempted to crawl away. He was walking the three blocks to his house from his job at a movie theater when he was ambushed on Bava Lane.

"No one will believe this, I know, but that guy's still out there, and he'll keep taking people down. I'll be scared to walk the streets when I get out of here. From now on, I'm taking the bus."

Police declined to comment on how seriously they are taking Swaggerty's account of events.

Section X

It was the best review we could have asked for. Peter Swaggerty had seen what we could do, and he was afraid.

Everyone was laughing at him, of course, and there would be no reappearance of this mysterious hybrid of Marvin the Martian and Edmond Kemper, but the skeptics would learn in time. It went like we'd hoped. Lee sculpted him, and Ursula and Geoff painted before and after representations of his violence to Swaggerty, whose routine they had noticed months ago. We probably didn't have to model the victim after a person we recognized, but to be on the safe side we did. Swaggerty might have invented the dialogue, but maybe that was the kind of thing a black silhouette with crazy eyes was born to say. Lee speculated that Blackie (as we called him) used Swaggerty as the author of his own pain. After that, we took more chances in preparation for our masterpiece. I gave my input on what we might utilize in these unorthodox manifestations, such as the neighborhood watch assailant (which had always haunted me as a child; being kidnapped was my worst fear), but I could contribute little else. Lee, Geoff, and Ursula worked tirelessly, and the experiments multiplied.

A steel incarnation of Baphomet showed up at a highly publicized environmentalist festival, resulting in the deaths of six at the hooves of the uninvited guest and another twelve trampled as by-standers fled, screaming in abject terror. Blood, it turns out, was not seen as very "green.'

A midnight screening of *Demons* was interrupted when a helicopter inexplicably crashed through the theater roof. Miraculously, the propellers continued whirling, and a full house was treated to the privilege of live decapitations and torso halving (provided they weren't the decapitatees and halvees). No crew members were ever found, nor was anyone ever able to determine where exactly the chopper had come from. That something almost identical happened in the movie was actually comforting to many, as though it proved it was simply a bizarre stunt rather than a paranormal phenomenon. No interpretations were offered for the letters EOTA painted on the side of the helicopter. The dream factory of the Gard Theater proved tragically cruel for another audience, some of whom were ground up in its cogs in something that would ultimately be called "the Gard Incident". A teenager texting a friend (about something nobody cared about even after what happened) suddenly stood up, shrieking that she couldn't see. Her boyfriend and another friend on her row came to her aid, while other jaded movie-goers told her to shut her trap. They needn't have worried. The friend (the recipient of the text, two seats away) held her illuminated cell phone screen up to the screaming girl's face. The faint blue glow revealed busy spools of blood gushing down her cheekbones. Her friends promptly joined her in a choir of ear-splitting hysteria (the boyfriend arguably more so). Someone else's makeshift cell phone flashlight added some unfortunate radiance to the macabre display, just in time for the spectators to get a better view as the girl's jaw suddenly unhinged from her skull. It was as though the integrity of her flesh and joints failed her instantaneously, the skin elongating like cheese from a slice of pizza. The weight of the jaw proved too much for the thinning strand, and the lower half of her face dropped to the floor of the auditorium. Now the screaming really began. By now, everybody close to this row had their cell phones trained on the cluster of the three of them. The girl with no mandible dropped back in her seat in a dead faint and, as one witness said, basically "exploded" on impact. Her head dropped one row back as if the top of her seat had been a samurai sword, and it careened into the lap of someone who hadn't had to get up from his seat to see the action, his free jumbo popcorn refills now a non-factor indeed. The trunk of her body splashed in myriad directions, a torrent of splatter like a tire shooting rain water up the side of a road. The friend, who now could have been a stand-in for Sissy Spacek in *Carrie* after the bucket dropped . . . if the bucket had been a bathtub . . . stood glued to the spot by the strange surplus of blood—surely far more than normally part of the human condition—unleashed from the bag of flesh with whom she'd entered this theater. Muscle memory even now allowed her fingers to walk on the keypad of her phone to inform somebody, anybody, that OMG, it was a massacre (to which she received the strange response "LOLZ" from an unknown number). She vomited from the sheer unthinkable horror. By this point, nobody was left standing around to play "best boy grip" with the surrogate lighting scheme, but the screen still provided enough light to see that the emesis was the color of the carpets in the atrium—a deep crimson. She instinctively reached for the (now ex) boyfriend, who was backing away from the tableau in what seemed like slow motion. He yanked his free hand away from the girl. Her hand came with him from the elbow down. He stopped backing away and *ran* for the end of the aisle, heedless of the debris of his ex-girlfriend still cluttering the way. The disembodied forearm burst beneath his shoe, and the backsplash of blood corroded his calves in quick succession. His momentum earned him one step, and then his leg wrenched itself away from the knee up, the foot still planted. It tipped over like an overloaded coat rack. He had nothing but the stump to come down upon, and as the now legless half of his body struck the seats to either side of him, he emulated the hot new trend of bodily decimation unwittingly started by his girlfriend. "Come on!" someone shouted above the chaos. *"Let's all go to the fucking lobby!"*

But nothing else happened. This virus or biological weapon or whatever it was seemed isolated to just the three of them. A government agency most of the general public had never heard of before shut the theater down and quarantined the auditorium. All of the ticketholders are still being examined at an undisclosed location while biological experts look for the elusive "Gard Factor," wishing to hell they'd gone to a matinee instead. (The "matinee" thing is conjecture, but the rest—right down to the line about the lobby, which I am proud to say was my own contribution— went directly as written, painted, and painstakingly sculpted over a series of weeks. I kept one of Lee's fragmented body sculptures . . . like a mini Han Solo in carbonite, dropped and shattered into tiny pieces.)

There seemed to be a lot of mass hysteria going around by that point. You would almost think it was a communicable disease with its own variation of a flu season. The barely repressed panic had returned. I was hearing it in conversations at work while I wrote pamphlets I did not comprehend. I was seeing it in the relief of my neighbors when they made it back to their apartments without being beaten and sodomized by a cartoon. It was in everybody's sudden mistrust of cell phones (and movie theaters), and the deep reluctance to go anywhere that a lot of people were gathered.

The success of the Gard Incident convinced it was time for our masterwork at last. We started by putting something different on the canvas and in the clay: ourselves.

Section XI

I agreed to go first, and the effect was instantaneous—needle-like punctures over my chest, like a mouthful of extended teeth perforating the skin. It looked like my heart had grown teeth and was attempting to gnaw itself out of me (see figure 11.1), with the ossific slivers simultaneously serving as an alien suture to seal the aperture. Such a disfiguration would disgust anyone who saw it, but Kathaaria changed all that.

Kathaaria was why Ursula wanted my contribution. My fascination with disease had impressed her with a vague poetic passion.

The results we wanted could not be adequately illustrated. Perhaps there could be a view of Earth as seen from space with mushroom clouds expanding all over, but why should we submit ourselves to such a conflagration? You can't imagine the plans we have for a world running on a different clock. So how do we really draw the rough beast slouching toward Bethlehem for those who won't be included? Well, along with Lee's molding of a triple-helix viral cell and Geoff and Ursula's portrayals of its effects, that is the purpose of this pamphlet. *The disease known as Kathaaria has a contagion rate of 100% among people without the deformity described above.*

Don't blame the messenger, but like I said, this never happened. It wasn't written, and you aren't reading it. It's after the end of the world. For those in the next one, though, the suffering we have shaped for you will be very real, as you will see described below in the *First Indications of Infection.*

Ryan Harding

AFTERMATH

A few words about each of the preceding stories, for those with a morbid curiosity.

Damaged Goods—I believe I stitched this together the night before I drove to Atlanta for the World Horror Convention in 1999, where my last minute planning resulted in sharing a hotel room with a couple of guys I hadn't actually talked to a whole lot before that point—Brian Keene and Mike Oliveri. Such were the benefits of being part of the Horrornet community, where even if you didn't always know somebody, you may as well have. I'm not sure what I would have come up with given slightly different circumstances, but I had read Lee & Pelan's *Shifters* shortly before this, and the whole "pizza cutter" scene communicated to me in no certain terms that I was going to have to go beyond the sensibilities of mere gore and bodily waste to make a real impression. That and a fairly steady diet of the hardcore solo offerings of Sir Lee at the time were integral to this metamorphosis. It was the best reception I ever got from a reading, before or since, and a lot of that was the payoff of no one knowing what to expect from me. The Gross Out Contest is sort of the exception to the rule about making a good first impression, or at least not "good" in the traditional sense. The judges were Richard Laymon, Jack Ketchum (who offered some choice commentary throughout the readings), John Pelan, and Simon Clark. "Damaged Goods" took first place. It is

more of a vignette than a short story due to trying to keep
time limit considerations for the reading. I have updated this
version to adjust continuity of later Von and Greg adventures
and lend a bit more gravitas . . . such as it is.

Sharing Needles—This was the last of the stories, written in
2003. I was invited to submit to an anthology called *Family
Plots*, where each story was to involve family members
committing a murder. I've been a true crime aficionado
since high school, and this seemed like a good opportunity to
explore that fascination. The challenge was to set up a story
where most of the internalizing came from journal entries
and the details emerged through the dialogue. Not exactly
"Bruce Willis was dead the whole time" as twist endings
go, but I still like it. As I recall, there were going to be 30+
contributors for *Family Plots* and it probably would have
been a logistical nightmare to get signatures from everyone
for a publisher based in Australia, but the publisher folded
and the project followed.

Genital Grinder: A Snuff Film in Five Acts—The World
Horror Convention in 2000 was held in Denver, and I
wanted to show up with something even more deranged. The
funny thing is that it wasn't originally going to be a sequel
to "Damaged Goods." I forgot about this until my friend
forwarded me an old email, but I was using the same concept
with different characters and a different tone. The problem
was that I had to be cognizant of a sensible time limit on
reading, and short of using an excerpt out of context I didn't
see how it was going to happen—it was taking too long to set
up. The easy solution was to use Von and Greg again. There
was a very different atmosphere to the Gross Out this time,
though, and by the time I read (I went last), the collective
interest was all but bled dry. I took 2nd to Mark McLaughlin,
a far more animated reader. The story did impress Kelly
Laymon, though, who wanted to put together an anthology
to use "Genital Grinder" as the closer. An amusing irony,
because I remember having an unemployment claim at the

154

time and being denied a shot at benefits for the week because the temp agency didn't deem the trip integral to my career. My college graduation would have been that weekend, but it wasn't a choice to me; I was going to read "Genital Grinder." This version of the story has been altered significantly and expanded by a few thousand words, once more for a new continuity and to embellish details I glossed over to have a more presentable story for a reading limit.

An additional fun fact to this is that Richard Laymon was once again a judge at WHC 2000, and asked me to mail a copy of the story to him. I was happy enough to do that with nothing expected in return—Richard Laymon asked me to send him my story!" was reward enough—but an "equal trade" for him was to send me copies of *The Travelling Vampire Show* and *A Writer's Tale*—hardcover editions

So not to have gone to WHC 2000, opting instead to do menial clerical tasks for a business that probably wouldn't have told me my time was up there until the very last day (just to make sure I didn't do a half-assed job at zero hour or, you know, actually contact my temp agency about finding me a new place to land immediately afterwards instead of having to wait for a new gig with no money coming in, which I've found is SOP for pretty much every single business that ever hired a temp) and go to a negligible graduation ceremony . . . I may as well never have written the story at all. I am pretty sure its appearance in Kelly Laymon's anthology for Freak Press is why this book is happening in the first place.

Laymon's note in The Travelling Vampire Show—*May all your travels lead to good things.*

See? Sometimes there's more to a story about a snuff movie than people being indiscriminately snuffed. Now, no one tell Peter Straub about the *Ghost Story* homage, okay?

Development—The story written for *In Laymon's Terms.* The deadline was running out on me (I actually still have the email I sent to Steve Gerlach asking that I not be disqualified for submitting because I didn't factor in the time difference in Australia), so I think I basically sat down and wrote all or the bulk of this in 10-12 hours on the last day left. This came before "Sharing Needles," and I think I was a bit obsessed with the "twist" possibilities from stories which used journals or dictations as a device. I had caught up to *Island* not long before this, and it was undoubtedly the biggest influence. Well, that and a chance remark from a friend with a job developing film about the kind of snapshots he was seeing on a daily basis. This was before the digital camera age really took over, and these days Carl would probably do his thing with a cell phone (if he could part with the money for one), so that's why I specifically tagged the journal entries with a year in this version. The irony of the marathon writing day needed to accomplish "Development" is that *In Laymon's Terms* would not actually be published for the better part of 10 years, so there was a time capsule sensibility to it when I finally got to read *ILT* in summer of 2011.

Emissary—The oldest of these stories, written sometime in the late 90s. I watched *Faces of Death IV* at a fairly impressionable age . . . impressionable enough to believe what I had seen was the real deal, no doubt about it. Years later I discovered otherwise, but those initial impressions lingered and are pretty much echoed by Gabriel in the story. Since I was determined to create stories out of the most extreme things I knew at the time, shockumentaries proved obvious fodder. I had a thing at the time for underdog characters being messengers of a greater calling, probably a byproduct of the Jaffe in Barker's *The Great and Secret Show*, a beginning that has always stayed with me. Of course, who can say Gabriel actually was or wasn't such a person? I'm not even sure.

Genital Grinder II: Dis-Membered—I don't know what I would have done if I couldn't have reassembled this story. To me, this was the ultimo Von and Greg adventure. Each section was written for a different bracket of an online gross-out tournament hosted by Delirium, grand prize being the publication of the winner's own short story collection and various Delirium titles for the ol' bookshelf. I had a few highlights mapped out in advance, but mostly it was written on the fly as needed for each new round. For reasons still unknown to me, I didn't save the story (but at least I still have that all important email to Steve Gerlach). I thought I had it stored on an email account, but no such luck, at least for all of it. I had parts 3 and 4. The computer I originally wrote it on was long gone, and it wasn't on any of the disks I had. I asked my friend Darrin if he still had it, because I had emailed him the installments before they went to the tournament. With help from his father, they found part 1 in addition to the aforementioned original Von and Gregless beginning to "Genital Grinder." Bob Strauss did the proofreading for the Delirium tournament, so I hit him up on the remote chance he might still have part 2 so many years later. He still had a hard copy, thankfully, and emailed me the scans of it. Now what would have been so hard about rewriting part 2 if he couldn't have provided it, you might wonder. Because apart from the initial dick robbery set-up and woman in the attic, I didn't remember very much of the story at all. It seems hard to believe that someone could forget reading some of these depravities, much less actually coming up with them in the first place, but that's what happened. I didn't remember there *was* a Slut Necro Lambda, and definitely not what exactly that might be.

As for the aforementioned attic scene, I had to read *Jayne Eyre* for a lit class in college, and some rather extreme commentary on the book suggested that Rochester hid his wife in the attic because she had syphilis. I thought that was something more befitting my own work when I chanced upon a picture of tertiary syphilis online one day.

I did end up winning the tournament, but Delirium temporarily went on hiatus shortly after and my collection was one of the casualties.

Final Indications—For a time, there were plans to do a Horrornet anthology with contributions by some of the various regulars. Brian Keene was going to be the editor. "Final Indications" was my entry. It never came to pass, unfortunately.

I was pleased when excavating it to discover I still liked it, since there was a time when I considered it my best short story. I've always said "extreme ideas" were as interesting to me as extreme fiction in general, which is why I always liked the cosmic horror of Lovecraft. This story probably shows a lot more influence in the way of Palahniuk and Ballard, though. When I was a kid, I used to think 2000 was going to be the end of it all. For some reason, I thought this was comforting. I had no such illusions when the time actually came. At 12:01 a.m. on January 1, 2000, I was watching Umberto Lenzi's *Cannibal Ferox* yet again, not expecting anything but a really bad time for Giovanni Lombardo Radice. The Y2K scare provided some interesting "human interest" stories in 1999, though, including one guy who I believe sold a lot of possessions to help fund a self-described "Mad Max" car for his family to have the advantage when it was time to pillage and plunder in the new dark age. At some point, I got to thinking about what someone who really believed in Armageddon would do when it didn't happen . . . and what if it happened and we didn't even know it.

***

This collection gave me the chance to go back and expand some of the ideas in these stories. In some cases they are a little longer than in their original (or intended) publication, while others are almost half again as long. A lot of names have been changed because I had a bad habit of using the same names a lot of times, and it was painfully obvious when the stories were all put together.

I hope to be back soon with other unseemly concepts, "bad ideas" in the grand Travis Bickle tradition. In my bios from publications, I used to tell readers to email me with the subject line "ARE YOU MORBID?" I'm still a big Celtic Frost fan (finally got to see them on the Monotheist tour), so you may do that at areyoustillmorbid@gmail.com. About 8 years since writing the oldest story here, the answer would still seem to be . . . yes.

RYAN HARDING is the co-author of the *Partners in Chyme* chapbook with Edward Lee. His stories have also appeared in the anthologies *In Laymon's Terms* and *Excitable Boys* and the chapbooks *A Darker Dawning* and *A Darker Dawning 2: Reign in Black.* Right now, he is probably either watching a film involving strange camera angles and a black-gloved killer or thinking about watching one.

deadite press

"Brain Cheese Buffet" Edward Lee - collecting nine of Lee's most sought after tales of violence and body fluids. Featuring the Stoker nominated "Mr. Torso," the legendary gross-out piece "The Dritiphilist," the notorious "The McCrath Model SS40-C, Series S," and six more stories to test your gag reflex.

"Edward Lee's writing is fast and mean as a chain saw revved to full-tilt boogie."
  - Jack Ketchum

"Bullet Through Your Face" Edward Lee - No writer is more extreme, perverted, or gross than Edward Lee. His world is one of psychopathic redneck rapists, sex addicted demons, and semen stealing aliens. Brace yourself, the king of splatterspunk is guaranteed to shock, offend, and make you laugh until you vomit.
"Lee pulls no punches."
  - Fangoria

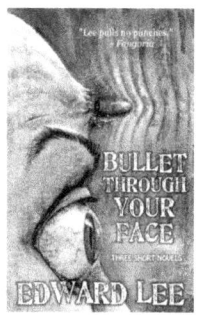

"Like Porno for Psychos" Wrath James White - From a world-ending orgy to home liposuction. From the hidden desires of politicians to a woman with a fetish for lions. This is a place where necrophilia, self-mutilation, and murder are all roads to love.

Like Porno for Psychos collects the most extreme erotic horror from the celebrated hardcore horror master. Wrath James White is your guide through sex, death, and the darkest desires of the heart.

"Trolley No. 1852" Edward Lee - In 1934, horror writer H.P. Lovecraft is invited to write a story for a subversive underground magazine, all on the condition that a pseudonym will be used. The pay is lofty, and God knows, Lovecraft needs the money. There's just one catch. It has to be a pornographic story . . . The 1852 Club is a bordello unlike any other. Its women are the most beautiful and they will do anything. But there is something else going on at this sex club. In the back rooms monsters are performing vile acts on each other and doors to other dimensions are opening . . .

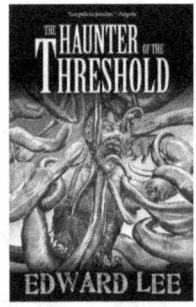

deadite press

"Urban Gothic" Brian Keene - When their car broke down in a dangerous inner-city neighborhood, Kerri and her friends thought they would find shelter inside an old, dark row home. They thought they would be safe there until help arrived. They were wrong. The residents who live down in the cellar and the tunnels beneath the city are far more dangerous than the streets outside, and they have a very special way of dealing with trespassers. Trapped in a world of darkness, populated by obscene abominations, they will have to fight back if they ever want to see the sun again.

"Ghoul" Brian Keene - There is something in the local cemetery that comes out at night. Something that is unearthing corpses and killing people. It's the summer of 1984 and Timmy and his friends are looking forward to no school, comic books, and adventure. But instead they will be fighting for their lives. The ghoul has smelled their blood and it is after them. But that's not the only monster they will face this summer . . . From award-winning horror master Brian Keene comes a novel of monsters, murder, and the loss of innocence.

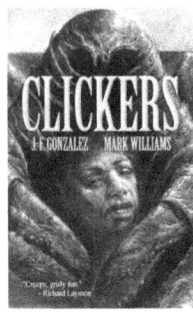

"Clickers" J. F. Gonzalez and Mark Williams- They are the Clickers, giant venomous blood-thirsty crabs from the depths of the sea. The only warning to their rampage of dismemberment and death is the terrible clicking of their claws. But these monsters aren't merely here to ravage and pillage. They are being driven onto land by fear. Something is hunting the Clickers. Something ancient and without mercy. *Clickers* is J. F. Gonzalez and Mark Williams' gore-soaked cult classic tribute to the giant monster B-movies of yesteryear.

"Clickers II" J. F. Gonzalez and Brian Keene- Thousands of Clickers swarm across the entire nation and march inland, slaughtering anyone and anything they come across. But this time the Clickers aren't blindly rushing onto land - they are being led by an intelligence older than civilization itself. A force that wants to take dry land away from the mammals. Those left alive soon realize that they must do everything and anything they can to protect humanity – no matter the cost. *This isn't war; this is extermination.*

"The Book of a Thousand Sins" Wrath James White - Welcome to a world of Zombie nymphomaniacs, psychopathic deities, voodoo surgery, and murderous priests. Where mutilation sex clubs are in vogue and torture machines are sex toys. No one makes it out alive – not even God himself.

"If Wrath James White doesn't make you cringe, you must be riding in the wrong end of a hearse."
-Jack Ketchum

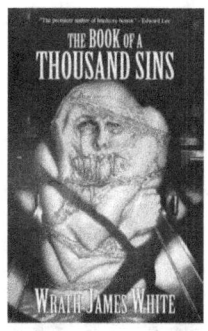

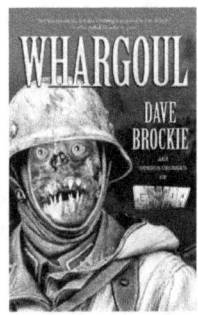

"Whargoul" Dave Brockie - It is a beast born in bullets and shrapnel, feeding off of pain, misery, and hard drugs. Cursed to wander the Earth without the hope of death, it is reborn again and again to spread the gospel of hate, abuse, and genocide. But what if it's not the only monster out there? What if there's something worse? From Dave Brockie, the twisted genius behind GWAR, comes a novel about the darkest days of the twentieth century.

"Take the Long Way Home" Brian Keene - All across the world, people suddenly vanish in the blink of an eye. Gone. Steve, Charlie and Frank were just trying to get home when it happened. Trapped in the ultimate traffic jam, they watch as civilization collapses, claiming the souls of those around them. God has called his faithful home, but the invitations for Steve, Charlie and Frank got lost. Now they must set off on foot through a nightmarish post-apocalyptic landscape in search of answers. In search of God. In search of their loved ones. And in search of home.

"Baby's First Book of Seriously Fucked-Up Shit" Robert Devereaux - From an orgy between God, Satan, Adam and Eve to beauty pageants for fetuses. From a giant human-absorbing tongue to a place where God is in the eyes of the psychopathic. This is a party at the furthest limits of human decency and cruelty. Robert Devereaux is your host but watch out, he's spiked the punch with drugs, sex, and dismemberment. Deadite Press is proud to present nine stories of the strange, the gross, and the just plain fucked up.

THE VERY BEST IN CULT HORROR

deadite press

"Zombies and Shit" Carlton Mellick III - Twenty people wake to find themselves in a boarded-up building in the middle of the zombie wasteland. They soon discover they have been chosen as contestants on a popular reality show called Zombie Survival. Each contestant is given a backpack of supplies and a unique weapon. Their goal: be the first to make it through the zombie-plagued city to the pickup zone alive. But because there's only one seat available on the helicopter, the contestants not only have to fight against the hordes of the living dead, they must also fight each other.

"Jack's Magic Beans" Brian Keene - It happens in a split-second. One moment, customers are happily shopping in the Save-A-Lot grocery store. The next instant, they are transformed into bloodthirsty psychotics, interested only in slaughtering one another and committing unimaginably atrocious and frenzied acts of violent depravity. Deadite Press is proud to bring one of Brian Keene's bleakest and most violent novellas back into print once more. This edition also includes four bonus short stories:

"Just Like Hell" Nate Southard- Dillion is a popular high school football star, gay, and tied to a chair in the dark. His lover is bound and gagged next to him. Around him are his teammates -- his captors. They aren't happy that they've been playing with a "faggot" and they intend to repay the disgrace. There will be humiliation, blood, and pain. But then it gets out of control. What started as black-hearted entertainment has turned into a cat-and-mouse game of gruesome justice. By the end of this night, four people will be dead. And those left alive will be forever scared.

"Depraved" Bryan Smith - Welcome to Hopkins Bend. You're never getting out of here alive... In the middle-of-nowhere, USA, there is a town not on any map. A place where outsiders are tortured, raped, and eaten. Where local law enforcement runs a sex trafficking ring. And the woods hold even more monstrous secrets. Today four unlucky travelers will end up in Hopkins Bend. If they want to ever get out alive they will have to become just as vicious and violent as their pursuers. Just as depraved.

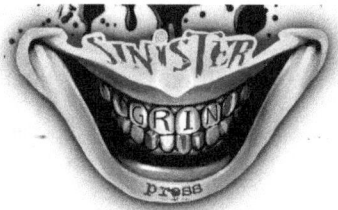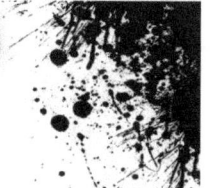

Horror That'll Carve a Smile on Your Face.

CUT CORNERS VOLUME 1
Ramsey Campbell, Bentley Little, & Ray Garton

Peel your eyes open, get comfortable, and let three of the horror genre's hardest hitters take you for a ride. Prepare yourselves, my friends, for you are placing your sanity in the hands of these masters of the macabre.

Three brand new stories guaranteed to slice open a smile.

SACRIFICE
Wrath James White

All over town, little girls are going missing and turning up starved, dehydrated, and nearly catatonic. One man is eaten alive by his own dog along with half the pets in the neighborhood. An elementary school teacher is beaten to death by his own students while being stung by thousands of bees. It's up to Detective John Malloy and his partner Detective Mohammed Rafik to figure out how it's all connected to a mysterious voodoo priestess with the power to take away all of your hatred ... all of your fear ... all of your pain.

THE KILLINGS
J.F. Gonzalez & Wrath James White

In 1911, Atlanta's African American community was terrorized by a serial killer that preyed on young bi-racial women, cutting their throats and mutilating their corpses. In the 1980s, more than twenty African American boys were murdered throughout Atlanta. In 2011, another string of sadistic murders have begun, and this time it's more brutal than ever. If Carmen Mendoza, an investigative reporter working for Atlanta's oldest newspaper, can solve the murders, she may find the key to ending the violent curse gripping Atlanta's Black community. If not, she might just become the next victim.

WWW.SINISTERGRINPRESS.COM

www.ingramcontent.com/pod-product-compliance
Lightning Source LLC
Chambersburg PA
CBHW051133260626
47170CB00005B/1800